WHEN KIDS TAKE OVER NASA

by Carole Marsh

GALLOPADE
INTERNATIONAL

Copyright 2011 by Carole Marsh
Gallopade International/Peachtree City, GA
First Edition
Ebook edition Copyright 2011

Published by Gallopade International/Carole Marsh Books
Printed in the United States of America.

Alley Way Books™ is the property of Carole Marsh
and Gallopade International.

Editor: Janice Baker
Research: Gabrielle Humphrey
Cover Design: Vicki DeJoy
Cover Photo: Anna Reuter
Content Design and Series Logo: Randolyn Friedlander

For all my grandkids: Christina, Grant, Avery, Ella, and Evan—
the world is my oyster...may the multiverse be yours!

Chaos is a theory that order always deteriorates into disorder...and that disorder always evolves into order.

The Butterfly Effect is, as an example, the fact that the flap of a butterfly's wing on one side of the world...can eventually lead to a tornado in Texas or a hurricane in Honduras...on the other side of the world.

Occam's Razor says that the simplest explanation is usually the right one.

Forthcoming

"When Kids Take Over" Books

When Kids Take Over the White House

When Kids Take Over Wall Street

When Kids Take Over Disney World

When Kids Take Over Congress

When Kids Take Over School

On June 8, 2011, schoolchildren everywhere watched large television screen monitors as the last American space shuttle lifted off the launch pad and headed into space. Like all launches during NASA's 30-year shuttle program, it was exciting, even if this one was not a nail-biter. Where once, even the thought of "going to space" thrilled the grandparents of these schoolchildren, the idea that the space shuttle era was over was mostly ho-hum, "So what?" or "No biggie" to many kids today. After all, there'd been 135 missions, and launches, to some people, had become routine. Of course, none of the school kids were old enough to have actually seen Neil Armstrong take that "one small step for man, one giant leap for mankind" earlier in the space program...nor shed tears as they watched with horror the shock of the explosion of Challenger and the death of the seven crew members on board, including schoolteacher Christa McAuliffe. But for NASA folks who were losing their jobs, for space junkies who were losing their shuttle launch fixes, and for five Houston kids who believed that they were losing their chance to go to space...well, it was a sorry state of *affairs and something they could not—and would not—accept. Alone, it was impossible. Together, it was a rip-roaring, space-snorting adventure. Would they get in trouble? OF COURSE!!!!!!*

AS AN APRICOT dawn spewed across Lake Nassau Pocket Park, a tiny green frog leaped energetically onto a dew-glistened lily pad. It was its nature to be up and about before dawn, peering around its habitat, lazily seeking its first drive-thru morning snack. This morning, the frog nabbed a fat mosquito as well as a perplexing long-distance view of some creature…a small white creature, which from the frog's perspective, was lifting forth from the horizon off a blossom of white and rising with the sun.

JOHN MASON WAS a habitual early bird, but this morning his young son, Mason, Jr., had thrown-up one chunk too many of pizza they'd had for dinner the night before. For that reason they were out and about tending to their morning dairy chores on their farm in Friendswood much later than usual.

John Mason had forgotten the date in the flurry of unanticipated cool washcloths and other comforting for his son. They were just wrangling the calves back to the barn when a distant rumble caught their exhausted attention. With a matching half-hunched turn of their right shoulders, they glanced around to observe, not the expected stray calf clambering across the rocky pasture, but a small, silvery speck in the sky appear to rise from the horizon and float upward like a glistening mote of dust.

The father lowered his large palm on his son's shoulder and squeezed gently. He spied the twin splotches of glow in the reflection of his son's upturned eyeglasses. They exchanged weary smiles and pressed on behind the mumbling calves wandering left and right to breakfast.

THE LAZY FLORIDA morning was like most others—hot and humid. For the official state marine mammal, the manatee, especially this one that was old, dented and bruised from encounters with random speedboats, morning was the same. The peachy-gray fog of dawn had parted like sour milk to reveal a clear blue sky streaked by peppermint. It's not as if a manatee is exactly a speedy creature, or particularly observant, or much cares what goes on up above the surface of the warm, nourishing, brackish water it hovers in. But still, it is God's creature and notes change. On this morning that change consisted of sturdy vibrations emanating from a distant bright gleam in the sky that reflected in the span of water over the manatee's lazily lapping fin. What the gleam was the manatee could neither know, nor care. That it was a historic event in its own right was irrelevant…after all, the manatee was a rather historic event itself, surviving for this long in these waters. The lumbering creature responded to the ambient alteration in its environment by flipping over and seeking shade in the cool water. Overhead, the thing blasted from the earth atop eyebrows of flame and a skirt of white foam, the din itself creating ripples on the water, which the manatee, now gone deep, ignored.

SOMEWHERE ON THE Space Coast, a region surrounding the Kennedy Space Center, a slow crawl of vehicles queued up in an irregular snake toward the destination of the launch of the last U.S. space shuttle. It was not the destination that mattered to the yawning, impatient occupants of these cars. After all, only the astronauts had a true front-row seat. And if you were not a NASA employee, major media network anchor, or VIP of some flavor or another, the view from this road, like many others roundabout, was "good enough."

Although the Johnsons had left their home before dawn, they were still stuck behind folks grabbing at Cheerios and bagels at the Titusville Hampton Inn. There was no rushing little Nattie anyway; she was only six, after all, but her father had thought this last launch historic enough that he took a day off from work (called in sick, actually) and trudged south from Waycross, Georgia, with his none-too-happy wife and sleepy-headed daughter to witness the event.

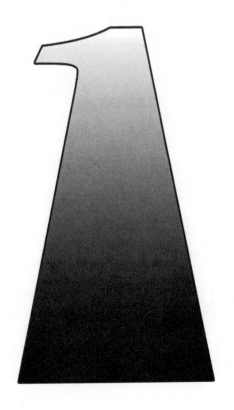

Liftoff!

WHEN KIDS TAKE OVER NASA

Christina's Story

The Fourth of July holiday had been great. I went with Mom, Dad, Mimi, Papa, aunts, uncles, cousins, and my brother Grant, of course—oh, bother—to Hilton Head Island, South Carolina. We got back just in time for a summer science class Grant and I took at a local college. Since we'd been gone for a week, I'd forgotten about the shuttle launch. I live in Houston and usually pay attention to space stuff. So I was surprised when the professor brought in her flat screen television from home so we could watch the launch of the last space shuttle. To me it looked a little like a trio of crayons—a fat burnt orange one between two skinny white ones. The massive metal gantries around the shuttle reminded me of orthodontia—at least until white smoke billowed out beneath the rockets. It was hard to believe that this was the last of the American space shuttles. I don't really quite understand that myself. Why? Money, probably—isn't everything these days? My grandmother writes about science stuff so I thought I'd email her and ask what's up. In our science lab, most of the kids just kept working on their projects, but I couldn't take my eyes off the launch. There's still something pretty amazing about seeing that big hulk of a spacecraft sitting there, then coming to life like some giant dragon and rip-roaring into space on a cloud of fire and smoke. It made me sad to think…*last launch…last launch*. So long, shuttle program. I just didn't see how this could be a good thing. But I had a project to finish, so I said a little prayer in my head for the astronauts and got back to work.

Grant's Story

I was in the same summer science class as my older sister, Christina. She thought I wasn't watching the launch, but I was. I'm a big space buff in a secret sort of way. My Uncle Michael had wanted to be in the space program back when he was in high school. He said advanced calculus did him in. I have a lot of friends whose moms or dads have been laid off since NASA's space shuttle program ended. I loved space camp as a little kid. Went to Space Academy in Huntsville, Alabama, last summer. So what gives? Isn't space important anymore? Didn't we learn a lot? Are we giving up? I mean I hear the Russians are still going space gangbusters. I don't get it. Gotta get back to my project— I want to beat my sister in the good grade race!

Kendall's Story

I'm disgusted. Is space obsolete now, or what? Am I supposed to grow old and tell my grandkids, "Oh, we decided we didn't need to go to space after all." It just seems like a critical mass of stupidity to me. Russia 1; America 0. "Hey, dudeskies, can we hitch a ride on your Mars Harley?" So what do we explore now: our bellybutton lint? Geez. How stupid can you get? You take something big like SPACE and, duh, you ignore it? Abandon it? Are adults idiots or what? The government sure seems shortsighted. Don't they figure that after we spoil all the water and poison all the food and other stuff and Ma Nature wipes out the rest…that we might need more than one single space station (one that I hear is pretty well dilapidated as it is) up there for us all to get on? Gonna be crowded! Oh, but no, it won't be…cause we can't get there! No shuttle, no more. I read private airplane companies would take over now. But they can only go so far and so fast—not to deep space. Besides, so only rich dudes get to go to space? Figures. I'm outta here.

Tica's Story

OK, so I'm little and Latina... get over it. Everyone treats me like I'm dumb because they almost automatically assume I'm an illegal immigrant. Big fat what they know, ya'll! I'm a naturally feisty person, I guess you could say...defensive... determined...I wanted to grow up and be an astronaut like the women I've seen on the space shuttle flights. But NOW...gee golly whiz...aren't we even going to Mars? Well, I am! I don't care what anybody else is doing. I AM GOING TO MARS! Gotta go... the launch is coming on television! So long, space shuttle—you're history! Hmm, no, maybe I don't want to go to space...I'll have to think about that. Would I have to wear a diaper for three years? Do spacesuits come in pink or denim? Can I wear my flip-flops?!

Jeremy's Story

I'm a kid. An orphan. In and out of the foster care system for forever. I just moved to Houston from Georgia not long ago. I don't know much about the space program, but it seems sort of exciting to live in the state where so much space stuff has happened. Must be some smart people here? My foster dad, Mr. Elliot, says he'll take me to Space Center Houston soon. But he won't. Will it even still be there? We watched the launch today; I was home sick. Mr. Elliot seemed mad about the shuttle program being scrapped. He said it was stupid and some other bad words. Who can understand adult stuff anyway? But space seems more about kids to me. We might go there one day, I hope! Live there? Maybe, maybe not? Maybe sooner, maybe later? Looks like later, much later. Gotta go…my nose is running in my PB&J—cool!

1

IT'S THE FIRST day of school, and somehow (later, they'd swear that the space fates did it), five kids: Christina, Grant, Kendall, Tica, and Jeremy—the same group that had shared an intense summer science camp—ended up in the same pre-college, advanced science class at a high school in Houston. Each have very different personalities, are ages 11-17, and aced all the tests that got them into this elite program. They do not mind being called nerds or geeks ("If the brain fits, wear it!" says Grant), but do not like to hear the other G-word: genius. They are each smart enough to know that IQ and SAT scores are only part of the smarts issue, and, that being smart is no insulation against the typical onslaught of adolescent issues. Smart and scared are not uncommon dorm mates.

It was one of those classes where you work on a main project as a team, as well as dividing up which parts you will do on your own. And being Houston, and being after the end of the shuttle program just a couple of months ago, and being everyone was pretty sick of hearing about it and all the economic repercussions, and being that their teacher was a Space Nut First Class, well, each project in the first session of this class was related to—one guess— duh, S P A C E!

"OK, you guys," said Ms. Rodriguez. She pointed at the five kids huddled around a beat-up old Rubik's Cube at one of the tables. "Your assignment...should you choose to accept it..." The kids booed the teacher's hokey reference to the old *Mission Impossible* television program. Besides, they didn't really get a choice of subject, just a "challenge," as Ms. Rodriguez liked to call it. (Later, five kids would recall her *Mission Impossible* joke with a different point of view.)

"YOUR CHALLENGE," the teacher addressed the five kids in a loud voice, "is to decide IF America should continue its space program now that the shuttle program's over...and if so (she grinned, knowing all the kids would think so), decide WHAT America should DO next, and WHEN, and HOW."

All the students in the class noted her emphasis on *America*, but knew she really meant NASA. Some kids at other tables groaned and you couldn't tell if they wished they'd gotten that assignment, or if they were glad they hadn't. Even though that team—Team Bonkers—tried to look cool, from their stretched back in chairs, slouched over notepads, fake bored, or other "I don't give a dadgum" positions, in one way or the other, they exchanged looks that gave away their surprise, satisfaction, and relief.

"At least we didn't get the CREATE A SPACE PORTA POTTY assignment," Kendall mumbled. The others giggled or nodded their heads in agreement.

Ms. Rodriguez turned away. "The packet of instructions for each team's assignment is on the table by the door. Get yours and get busy. As always in this class, you can tackle your assignment any way you wish…here, offsite, at home, the library. You know the drill. But there is a deadline: all assignments must be completed for show and tell by September 15. There will not be a test, of course, but you will get an individual grade and a team grade. The top scoring team will be recognized during honor's day next spring. Also, maybe some of you will go to the state science fair, or even the national science fair. And scholarships are always lurking out there for brilliant kids doing brilliant jobs. You know how to reach me. Good luck."

Ms. Rodriguez turned on a well-worn, three-inch stacked heel and left the room. For all they knew, having been in her Special Assignments Class before, they would not see her again until it was time to turn in their projects. She was notorious for vanishing, and they all believed that was her way of leaving them to sink or swim. Probably, they believed, she was somewhere working on their next assignment—she had a million of them—all harder and more challenging than the next. That's why this was their favorite class—by far.

After all, there they were: officially out of class for the week, in control, on their own...and glad to be so. *What WAS that teacher thinkin'?!*

The National Oceanic and Atmospheric Administration's National Hurricane Center reports a tropical depression has formed off the west coast of Africa. Stay tuned to this weather channel for further information...

2

It was a shark gray day. Half the school—students and teachers—seemed to be out with the flu. Already! Just a week before, when school started, it had been the end of one of the hottest summers on record in Houston. Drought. Dust. Hot. Endless days above 90—then 100—degrees.

Of course, as usual during the June-to-November hurricane season, the National Weather Center regularly blared warnings of the latest tropical depression far out in the Atlantic Ocean—an unending, repetitious, weather radio get-on-your-nerves tracking of the longitude and latitude of any batch of wind that might eventually adopt the Butterfly Effect and ram itself into the Gulf Coast, like Hurricane Irene just had.

One kid in the Special Assignments Class was so hurricane crazy he'd named his dog and cat Saffir and Simpson after the Hurricane Wind Scale. Not everyone in Houston was all NASA all the time, just the self-professed space geeks, of which

all five members of Team Bonkers were…
absolutely…in spades.

The day's unsettled weather, and
more than a few, uh, personal problems
had Team Bonkers members bored, tired,
and cranky.

It was obvious that they were out of
sorts, or they'd have been anywhere but the
Special Assignment classroom. Anywhere.
After all, what good is a free-ranging class if
you stick around the classroom?

They were the only team at their table
this dreary afternoon. Slumped on elbows
and doodling on legal pads, they pushed
and shoved one another, burped, grumbled,
and otherwise acted like the frustrated kids
they were.

"Our deadline is not that far away," said
Christina. She felt like a human barometer
with the blood in her veins burbling up and
down with the changing weather pattern.
At the beach this summer, she'd even been
able to tell when it was high or low tide by
the feeling she had inside. "We need a plan."
She twisted the end of one of her long,
brown strands of hair—a habit when she
was tense.

Tall and slim, Christina was the oldest of the group, but she never rubbed it in. Maturity was an elusive thing, she'd discovered, and it was easier to be wrong if you didn't try to show off you were right all the time. Some of the other Special Assignments teams were full of big egos, and she was glad her team wasn't. *Her team*...she knew she'd better be careful with that term. She glanced over at Kendall, one year younger, awfully smart, and awfully good-looking for a geek.

"We need summer back," grumbled Kendall. He had a pencil stuck behind his ear and was scribbling on a yellow ruled notepad. He kept rubbing his hand over his head, his nervous I'm-thinking-but-stumped habit.

"I need a chili dog," said Grant, rubbing his stomach. He was always hungry, always disheveled, and mostly always in some kind of trouble or another because he was so silly and a prankster. Still, Christina had to admit he was a sweet brother, almost too good sometimes, very sensitive—he loved to eat fish, for example, but didn't think you should kill them. He was also a big ham every chance he got, and when he didn't get a chance—he just created one.

Grant hung over Tica's shoulder. "Whatcha doin', show-off? You got an idea yet? Spit it out."

"NONE…of…your…BUSINESS!" Tica said, elbowing him right off his wooden stool.

"Ouch!" screeched Grant in mock pain as he theatrically rolled on the floor holding his sides.

"No, really, Tica," said Christina in a deadpan voice. "What are you working on? Team Bonkers is usually rappin' with ideas, but we are in a brain fog. Must be the weather and withdrawal symptoms from summer being over. Or," Christina added with a bad feeling, "we are coming down with whatever's already going around school."

"Hmmmph!" huffed Tica. "What did you do this summer?"

"Went hiking in Colorado!" Grant answered. He jumped up and spread his arms and legs in a mountain hiking mode and pretended to charge up a steep cliff then rappel back down.

"Went to see Grandma on North Carolina's Outer Banks," groaned Kendall. "I musta ate a hog's worth of barbecue, Brunswick stew, hushpuppies, and peach cobbler...man, that woman can cook!"

Tica *hmmmphed* again. "Well, I stayed home while my mama cleaned toilets over at the civic center. So I had plenty of time to *think*."

"What did you think about?" Jeremy asked gently. Everyone knew he lived in a foster home and did not like it. Jeremy was quiet, and friendly, but he never smiled. With no parents, or other relatives, the boy had plenty of reason to be sad, but mostly he acted happy, just never smiled.

Worst of all, Christina thought (though she felt bad to feel this way), he was so smart. But when he turned eighteen, her mother told her, he would "age out" of the foster care system with no money and no place to go. Of course, since he was the youngest of their group, that wouldn't be for a few years.

Christina was already conspiring with Grant on how they might keep Jeremy, who she knew was not some rescue pup, and would be too independent to go for such a plan. No, he'd work his way through college if he could. But what the poor boy really needed most, she knew, came from the heart. She'd never told him she loved him like a little brother. Maybe she should.

What a motley crew, Christina thought to herself. This was a great school with a lot of good teachers and kids, but she knew a lot of kids with problems of all kinds. In various ways, each Team Bonkers member fell into that category. Maybe all kids did, she suspected, even cool, popular kids who pretended things were perfect. Just watch the news. Read the newspaper. What was "normal" anyway? Who even knew, she thought, who knew?

Tica was an immigrant from Mexico. While she insisted she was legal, Christina was not so sure about that. She felt Tica did "protest too much." Christina's dad warned her to stay out of it, if she cared about Tica.

"Sometimes too much information is…uh, too much information," he'd told her and Grant cryptically. Yeah, they conspired to take in Tica, too, even though she was one spicy handful. You didn't mess with

Tica! She was a pit bull in denim skirts and tight pink tank tops. Oh, yeah, and flip-flops. Always flip-flops.

"I saw it, Tica! I saw it!" Christina said, pounding the table suddenly with her fist. "You smiled! You've got an idea, I know it. WE know it! You don't show your pearly whites ever *unless*..."

"Shut up your pie hole!" Tica said, grinning broadly. With the same swipe of her hand she used on her ever-present iPhone, she spun her legal pad around so the others could see.

3

The kids stared intently at Tica's rough sketches.

"It's a, uh, uh, a washing machine?" guessed Kendall, but he was grinning too.

"Is not!" said Tica.

"It's a rocket ship," said Christina, matter-of-factly.

"What an old-fashioned term, sis," Grant exclaimed. "What are you, a Neanderthal from the last gallinium?"

Christina frowned and continued to stare at the sketch.

"It's the shuttle, isn't it?" guessed Kendall. "The one that just went up, right?"

Tica shook her head no.

Jeremy turned the page toward him. He was the kind of kid who had little to say but when he said it you listened. Finally he drawled in a soft, wistful voice, "It's a launch, isn't it?" He didn't look up for an answer. "A new shuttle. One we build. One we launch. It's our project." He looked up. He was not smiling. He was not even asking a question. He and Tica just stared at each other.

"Well, bad words!" snarled Kendall. "Nice idea, dudes, but the shuttle has left the building: Kaput! Gone bye-bye! Canceled! Deep-sixed!" He rubbed his forehead in disgust.

"Exactly!" said Christina. She grabbed for the pad. "But our project is about the future. And we can talk about it, or write about it, or draw it…but what if we DID IT?!"

"Did what?" Kendall demanded, swiping his hand through his dark hair. "Dream pie-in-the-sky, EXCUSE ME…pie-in-space dreams that aren't possible. Grade Z for us, Bonkers."

They all knew Kendall. The angrier and louder he got, the more in denial, the more filled with insults, angst, and indignation, the more he was buying into an idea. Suddenly, he reached across the table and grabbed Tica by the neck in a mock chokehold. *"WHEN?"* he screamed in her face, *"do we start?"*

4

They started at a bar—the Smoke from a Distant Star bar. It was where some of the unemployed, disgruntled, disgusted, and discouraged former NASA workers hung out.

Christina was the only one old enough to drive, besides Kendall, who didn't have his permit yet. He didn't have a car, anyway, and she only had a real jalopy of a Mustang her mom had driven way back in college.

They needed to get to the part of town they were determined to visit. And, they needed to go after school and still get back before anyone realized that they weren't just staying after school to study. It would be a tight squeeze in the Houston rush-hour traffic, especially with talk of a potential tropical storm.

No matter how premature the storm warnings, many people would still dash out to get milk and bread and fill up with gas. Sort of silly, Christina thought, when the storm was still far out in the Atlantic and there was no telling if it would actually ever turn into a hurricane or, even if it did, come their direction. But Hurricane Katrina had changed everything.

Christina and Grant's parents were both working late. Tica's mom worked her second job in the afternoons and evenings. No one would look for or worry about where Jeremy was. And Kendall? Well, it was his father they were in search of at the bar.

Christina headed down I-45 South, merging with the throng of vehicles inching onto the highway ahead of her. As she nervously navigated the stop-and-go traffic towards the NASA 1 Bypass exit the other kids jabbered on and on about nothing. They also ran the car windows up and down, turned the radio up and down, and talked loud or louder, otherwise driving her crazy.

"Hush, you guys!" she pleaded. "I'm trying to think."

"Don't think," said Grant, "drive!"
Christina then did something that surprised them all. After exiting the highway, she clicked on the car's flashers and found a safe place to stop.

"Look, you guys, this is no joy ride," she began, twisting around so they each could see the perturbed look on her face. "Pipe down and help me find this place or I promise…I will drop you all at the nearest bus station and leave you there."

They could tell Christina wasn't kidding. Her usually tidy hair was unraveling against her sweaty brow. Her hands shook on the steering wheel. She had only been driving since the first of the year, and seldom on the interstate. Actually, she preferred to drive their golf cart more than the car.

"Houston, we have a problem," Grant said softly and hung his head. "Sure, sis, got it, over and out." He saluted.

"Behavin' now," promised Tica. "We are, Christina—promise."

Kendall nodded. He turned off the radio squawking about likely afternoon thunderstorms.

"Put your seat belt on too," Christina said coldly, giving Kendall a "you'd better" glare. She did not want to ever cause someone to get hurt in a car wreck, least of all herself. She knew the kids knew better than to act like this. They were just excited and giddy with rare actual disobedience from an SAT off-the-chart group. Finally, she exhaled loudly, and switching from flashers to left turn signal, carefully pulled back onto NASA Parkway.

"Help out, Kendall," Christina ordered. She knew the Baybrook Mall and the Friendswood area were just behind them now, so she was trying to keep an eye out for Clearwater Lake.

Kendall had Googled a Johnson Space Center area map and was trying to make heads or tails out of the snarl of roads, all with corny out-of-this-world names like NASA Road, Saturn Way, and Space Center Boulevard.

"Hey, it says this place was established in 1961 as the Manned Spacecraft Center. In 1973 it was renamed the Johnson Space Center after President Lyndon B. Johnson who was from Texas. Remember him?—big hat, big nose, big ears, the president big on civil rights, and space. I guess, anyway."

"Honestly, Kendall, I don't care about all that right now," Christina said. "See if you can spot which road we take, please." Her hands tightly gripped the steering wheel. Kendall nodded.

As the skies grew darker, and other car lights blipped on with the first fat spatter of raindrops, Christina dared not take her eyes off the road. Finally, Kendall pointed to Clearwater Lake on the map. "OK! Saturn Lane should be up here on the left," he informed her.

Christina finally made her way through the maze of roads that led to the Smoke from a Distant Star bar. As she pulled into the parking lot, gravel crunched beneath her tires like granola.

"At least there are no adults or cops in the parking lot," said Tica. "A carful of school kids has gotta look pretty suspicious. Just on a Sunday drive, is that what we'd say? Ha!"

"It's not Sunday," Jeremy said.

"Hush, Tica!" warned the others, used to her incessant diatribe over what bad things might happen, even in the best and most innocent of circumstances, and this was far from either of those.

Christina glanced at her iPhone. It was six o'clock "straight-up," like a drink without ice, she thought. Instead of being at home doing homework, here they were smack in the middle of happy hour or misery hour or whatever they called it. She gave Kendall a questioning look. This had been his hair-brained idea and now she was unsure why they were here or what they were supposed to do.

Naturally, kids younger than legal age weren't allowed in a bar, but as always, Team Bonkers had a scheme.

"Christina, you go in and say you are looking for your father, that he's needed at home," instructed Kendall.

"And when they ask me who my dad is, what do I say?" Christina asked, giving Kendall an odd look.

Grant snapped his fingers. "Say Grant Kendall!"

His sister shrugged.

"Well, what do we do?" asked Tica.

"Once Christina goes in and gets the barflies occupied with looking for her non-existent drunk dad, we go in and claim we're here to get her out of there and bring her home," said Kendall.

"Why all this subterfuge?" asked Tica.

"One reason," said Kendall. "We need a guy named Carl to come outside."

"How do you know he will?" asked Christina.

Kendall shrugged. "Cause he's a really nice guy," he said in a facetious tone. "A real drunk, so he won't remember later, which is important, but I guarantee he will be the one to escort us kids out. He likes to be in charge. He might look mean but that will just be show for the other guys in the bar. It'll be OK." He looked desperate for them to understand and agree.

Christina shook her head. "Oh, brother, Kendall. And how do you know this Carl will just shuttle us out of the bar and not offer us a drink or call the cops or…"

Kendall shoved his face into hers. "Because he's my dad!"

Christina took a step back. No one said a word until Grant asked, "But why do we need him to do our school project?"

Kendall blushed and shrugged. "We don't. My dad was in charge of facilities at Johnson Space Center…and he had a set of keys to the joint. He still does. I know. I think he made a secret copy of them before he was laid off. I see him lay it on his bedside table every night. That is, when he's home."

"*Ohhhhh,*" the other kids said together.

Christina had been suspicious when Kendall had suggested—actually insisted—that they come to this bar with no questions asked. She'd had an idea it was about his father, whom he seldom mentioned, so she was not surprised to have been right. Still, this seemed risky. But *keys* to the Johnson Space Center?! She knew they weren't gonna turn down getting their hands on those, though to do what with them exactly, she had no idea.

Christina hopped out of the car with a long-legged, confident stride she didn't feel in her bones and paraded through the light rain up to the door before anyone could stop her.

Once inside she was surprised to be temporarily blinded in the dim light. Maybe what she didn't actually see wouldn't hurt her, she hoped. So in a loud, and as obnoxious a voice as she could muster, she squealed, "I need my dad! He's needed at home! Anybody seen, uh (the pause produced a snicker from an unseen man at the bar), uh, Grant Kendall? MISTER Grant Kendall."

Instantly, Christina's fake bravado failed her. She had that fight or flight feeling and was ready to run, her face red with embarrassment.

They should have sent in Tica, she realized too late, who would have been great at this charade. She waited for laughter at her exhibition, but instead there was a mumble of voices and a rustle of movement in the dusky bar backlit by pink and lime neon signs. Christina just stood there, waiting.

In the next moment, the other kids fell inside the bar from the door where they'd been listening.

"Christina! Get out of here now!" Kendall called out in an aggravated voice, as if he had to chase the poor girl out of bars all the time. But Christina was frozen in place. She didn't know what to do—but Carl Crispin did.

Just as Kendall had predicted, his dad, with a scowl on his day-old bearded face, did indeed escort the kids out of the bar, to hoots and hollers of the other patrons.

Once outside, he laughed and scrubbed his knuckles through his son's hair. "Yo, son, wha you kli, I mean kids, do doin' wha…good to see…" Kendall's dad slurred as he staggered down the wet steps, almost falling.

With a deep blush, Kendall took his father by the arm of his ragged, stained NASA tee shirt and helped him to a nearby rusting metal stool propped against the side of the building. The drizzle was lessening but they were all still getting wet, which felt miserable in the thick Houston humidity.

"Good to see you, too, Dad," Kendall said, but not in a tone of voice that in any way sounded genuine. "These are my friends. We just wanted to say hello. Why don't you go back inside now, Dad, OK?" He helped his father stand up and steered him back toward the entrance of the bar.

His father gave him a sloppy hug. "Frens…frens…nice, Kenny, nice…" he said and vanished back into the bar.

"Well, dang!" said Tica. "What did that accomplish? All that song and dance and all you do is smooch up your dad and send him back to perdition, Kendall? What…"

"Shut up," Kendall said sharply. He held up his hand and opened it.

The other kids stared at the fat ring of keys and then at Kendall.

"Well, ding, dang, dong!" said Tica.

The National Oceanic and Atmospheric Administration's National Hurricane Center reports Tropical Depression #10 was upgraded to a Tropical Storm at 4PM CDT today. The storm became better organized as it passed over the Cape Verde Islands in the Central Atlantic Ocean. Stay tuned to this weather channel for further information...

S

Although the rain had stopped, streaks of lightning staggered around on the horizon. A three-quarters moon nestled lazily in a cottony clot of cloud overhead. It peered out only long enough to ponder the five kids huddled before the hulk of the Johnson Space Center. Surrounded by fence, darkness, and only a lone, distant pink security light shrouded in low fog, the buildings looked abandoned, ashamed, lost.

Sometime after the shuttle shutdown, the Johnson Space Center had been closed down "indefinitely." It seemed strange to see such a once busy place so dark and lonesome. The enormous locks on the main entrance gate looked forbidding. The huge parking lot was empty. Not a single security guard was in sight.

Afraid to go in the main gate, Christina drove around the side of the Johnson Space Center complex and discovered a piece of fence peeled back just enough for the car to get through. She parked between two small structures. Quickly, they waded through oily puddles to the front of the Johnson Space Center's main building. "We shouldn't do this," said Christina in a muffled voice.

"Use the key!" Grant urged, giving Kendall's elbow a nudge. "Use it now before we lose our nerve."

"Or before the cops show up!" said Tica.

Lost in his own thoughts, Jeremy just stared up at the enormous building looming before them.

"OK, OK!" said Kendall, "but I only have a key for the back door. Come on!"

Clinging close to the fence, the kids hurried around the building—one of a large complex of buildings of all sizes. Stooping low, and hoping not to be seen, they made a beeline to the lone steel back door. It unlocked easily with the key Kendall clutched in his sweaty hand and the kids slipped inside.

Low wattage emergency lights gave an eerie glow to the inside of the building and the kids stood there for a minute while their eyes adjusted.

"Oh, ghosts of astronauts past..." muttered Jeremy.

"Knock it off, Jeremy!" groused Kendall. "No kidding about stuff like that, will ya."

Jeremy gave Kendall a curious look. "But I wasn't kidding, Ken. Can't you feel them? I can."

Kendall responded by stalking off down the hall.

"I thought there'd be some fancy reception area," said Tica, looking at the antiseptic, hospital-like wide corridors.

"We came in the back door, remember," Grant said. "Just utilitarian stuff. The big, pretty tourist welcome area is probably on the other side of this humongous building."

Christina sighed. She stood in the hallway with her arms folded, a curl of her dark hair circled over a corner of one blue eye. "I think we should decide what we're doing here," she said. "I didn't want to come just for a tour."

Kendall had wandered back down the hallway. "Then follow me," he said, turning on his heel.

The kids traipsed after him into an ordinary small conference room, one probably used for quick meetings or interviews, they figured.

"I think we can sit here and decide what to do next," said Kendall with a baleful look at Christina.

"I just think we need a PLAN," huffed Christina. "More than just the sketchy ideas we had back at school." She gave Tica an apologetic look.

"Me, too," said Grant.

The kids scrambled into seats.

"So what is our biggie-do project *now*?" said Tica.

"I think we should launch our own rocket," Jeremy said calmly.

"On purpose?" asked Tica. She slapped her hands against her cheeks in mock shock.

"Maybe we should pick a more realistic project," Christina suggested.

"Why?" said Kendall. "Did we really break into the Johnson Space Center just to write a report?"

"We didn't break in," Grant reminded them. "We had a key."

"Right, buddy, sure, tell the cops!" said Tica with a laugh.

Then the kids grew quiet.

"What started this was that we all thought America should continue its space program," Christina reminded them.

"So let's help," Jeremy said, again, very calmly but with a resoluteness that worried Christina.

Kendall doodled on the table with a finger. "Since we're in here, there's no harm in pretending we'd launch a real mission. We could each take on a role and then spend some time doing research and moving a plan along as far as we can. Just as if we were really going all the way to launch."

"Can we use the zero-gravity-amusement-ride-thing-a-ma-bob?" Grant asked eagerly.

"No we cannot!" said Christina. "It's not a ride and that idea is not amusing. Space science is serious stuff. We can't kid around here or someone will get hurt, guys."

The others stared at her, wondering why she was taking things so seriously and squeezing the fun out of everything. She knew them all well enough to know that they were just nervous and horsing around. They were quiet for a couple of minutes. Christina was the first to break the silence.

"Okay, then, if that's how it is…I'll be the CapCom. I always wanted to," she added wistfully.

Kendall lunged across the table at her. "No way! I want to be CapCom. Pick something else! When was a girl ever the Capsule Communicator anyway?"

Christina and Tica burst out laughing.

"Uh, sexist dude, this is today's NASA… we girls can—and will—do anything," said Tica, with a flounce of her dark hair.

"Besides," added Christina, tugging something out of her backpack, "I have a CapCom hat!" She slapped it on her head and the other kids gasped.

"Hey, sis, you got that light years ago when we came here for Space Camp," marveled Grant. "Can't believe you still have it."

Christina ripped off the hat and looked at it fondly. "It's been through the washer once too often, but I could never get rid of it." She put the cap back on with a tender tug.

"Good thing," Jeremy said seriously to Christina, but he was staring at Kendall.

"Geez…OK, OK," Kendall said. "You be CapCom. I'll work on the propulsion system. A rocket that can't go anywhere is just a hunka junk."

"Good deal!" said Grant. "I will be the go-fer."

"The WHAT?" said Tica. "I never heard of no space job called gopher."

Grant giggled. "There's always a go-fer. You guys will need a lot of different stuff and I can go-fer it and speed things up. I'll do stuff too, but that way…"

"We get it! We get it!" Kendall said, though Tica still looked puzzled.

"Well, you look like a gopher, I guess," Tica said, and everyone except Grant laughed.

Suddenly, Tica snapped her fingers. "I'll be a specialist. There are always special things to hunker down and get done and I can do those tasks."

"Like make burgers and fries?" Grant asked in all sincerity, so he was pretty shocked when Tica literally jumped on his head, causing him to yowl.

"Shhhh...shhhhh!" warned the other kids.

"Grant WAS just kidding, Tica," Christina said.

Her brother rubbed his head as Tica backed off. "No, I really wasn't," he admitted. "I'm just hungry. Aren't you guys?"

"I'll be a SIM SUP then," Tica said, dreamily, ignoring Grant. "That's a simulation supervisor, if ya'll want to know. I'll train astronauts. I'll dunk them in that water tank that simulates zero gravity and spin them around in the centrifugal what-cha-ma-call-it Vomit Comet thing. I'll..."

"That's a great idea," Christina assured Tica to hush her up.

"There's gotta be a canteen around here somewhere," said Kendall, hopping up. "Like a rocket, we need fuel to work. Come on."

As they left the room, Christina turned to Jeremy. "What are you going to do?" she asked him.

"Don't worry about it," Jeremy said. "There's a lot to do. I'll find something."

With the sound of a distant yelp they realized that Grant had discovered the canteen. But when they all got to it, they discovered that it had clearly been cleaned up and closed for business. But in a few minutes, Kendall had plugged in the microwave and the scent of some frozen MRE's wafted through the building. It was all they could find—some old military Meals Ready to Eat…but they were starving.

As they shared the glop that came out of the packages, Jeremy hung back by the door. "Smell good, ghosts of astronauts past?" he whispered. He had learned to keep most of his thoughts and comments to himself. Safer that way. No sense upsetting, or outright scaring anyone. After all, he needed their help.

7

Within the hour, long before they really wanted to leave and before they even had a chance to explore, the kids cleaned up their MRE mess and left the building. Kendall carefully checked to see that all looked just the way they had found it.

"We are so running late!" moaned Christina. "We've got to get home."

"Some of us," muttered Jeremy.

Checking for any security guard, the kids carefully made their way back to the car. Christina slowly wove her way past the buildings and out the side gate they'd left open just enough to escape quickly if they'd needed to.

As they passed various Johnson Space Center buildings, they read the intriguing names. In an almost reverent tone, Jeremy chanted: "Foreign Object Debris...Neutral Buoyancy Lab...Building Eight..."

Even the buildings that were just mysteriously numbered, not named, enthralled them. What was inside? What happened there? Could they get inside?

Kendall read the street names aloud, partly to help Christina navigate her way back to the interstate and partly just to hear them: "Challenger Parkway....Aerospace Boulevard...Saturn Lane...Space Center Boulevard..."

As they drove down the interstate, Grant was more interested in noting "Jack In the Box...Sonic...Subway...Angelo's Pizza..." The others groaned. "What?" asked Grant unhappily. "I'm a growing boy. I'm still hungry." He sat back and droned on: "Quiznos...Fuddruckers...McDonald's... Wendy's..."

"NASA workers must love fast food," Tica noted.

"We'll eat some more when we get home," Christina promised her brother. At the thought of home they all grew quiet, wondering how they could manage their project with the Johnson Space Center so far away, school, parents, homework, and way too many other issues. They had no idea that even as they drove toward home, the space fates were at work to help them out yet again.

One by one, Christina dropped off the other kids.

Tica's mom was still at work. Kendall's dad was still at the bar, of course. Jeremy reluctantly got out of the car; Christina was not even certain that he would go into his foster home, which was dark anyway.

When she and Grant got home, their parents were still out at a meeting, so they were able to slip in and settle down as if they'd been doing homework for a long time.

Although Christina knew that they couldn't take a jaunt out to Johnson Space Center every afternoon, she just couldn't think about it anymore tonight. Grant raided the fridge for any leftovers. Christina fell asleep over her advanced calculus.

9

As it turned out, they didn't have to sneak from school to the Johnson Space Center each afternoon after all.

Tica's mother was given a promotion by her cleaning service. They wanted to send her to Austin for training on how to clean sensitive equipment, the kind in clean rooms, hospital laboratories, and computer database centers. At first she told them that she absolutely could not go. She explained that she had a child she could not pull out of school, and she had no one to care for her while she was away. Tica had told her mother that she could stay with Christina. "Christina's mom says so!" Tica fibbed, fingers crossed behind her back, crossed for good luck that maybe she really could. Tica's mother had believed her and taken the next bus to Austin so as not to miss the training orientation. She would not be back for two weeks.

Kendall's dad was no problem; he would never have known if his son was at home or on the Moon anyway. His mom might have been an issue, but she'd had it with the whole drinking scene and just after school started, she had left to live with her mother in San Antonio. She'd given her son a chance to choose whether to come with her or stay with his father. Kendall had chosen to stay in Houston "because of school" he made sure his mother knew. She was not surprised.

Christina and Grant were startled the next morning when their parents told them that the meeting they'd been to regarded an emergency two-week trip to Africa to document an outbreak of the dreaded Ebola disease. Both their mom and dad worked for the CDC, the Centers for Disease Control, out of a Houston office. Their specialty— infectious diseases—was the same, so this was a rare opportunity. They had already called Grandma Mimi in Georgia to see if she could come and stay with the kids while they were gone. They had to leave immediately. As usual, when things like this came up—"opportunities" Mom always called them, "obligations" is how their father referred to them—they tried not to show their adrenaline rush. Indeed, their parents actually tried to act somber and forlorn that they would have to leave. However, Christina and Grant always felt (and more or less understood) their mom and dad's extreme excitement over germs that can kill up to ninety percent of people they infect in a very short time, in a horrible "bleed out" way. As Christina and Grant got ready for school, their parents called a taxi and left for the airport. They later landed at Andrews Air Force Base outside of Washington, DC, and then were quickly on their way across the Atlantic Ocean on a special charter flight to Kinshasa. Just before Christina and Grant left the house, the phone rang. It was their grandmother. She was calling from Piedmont Hospital in Atlanta and said, "I fell! I broke my hip! I'm about to have surgery! Tell your parents I'll get there as soon as I can!" She was in tears; her grandkids were sad for her. Grant, who had answered the phone, insisted, "It's OK, Mimi. We'll be OK. You get well…" and after he hung up, added "but not for a couple of weeks, please."

Jeremy was no problem. He did go in the Brookings Home for Kids the night before, where Mr. Elliot belted him one for being so late. A tooth was knocked out. Jeremy put it in his pocket and stuffed the hole in his gum with toilet paper. Then he packed a small, cheap suitcase with all he owned and began to haul it—and his teddy bear—around with him everywhere he went, including to school the next day.

10

When they met up at school, the kids were astounded to discover the incredible star alignment that led to them being, presumably, home free, parent free, "Scott free!" said Kendall (though Grant wondered who the heck Scott was) for approximately... hopefully...PLEASE! PLEASE! PLEASE! the next two weeks.

If they had ever had misgivings about their vague concept of breaking into the Johnson Space Center and seeing what they could do to revive the space program—on paper, at least—most of them no longer had any qualms whatsoever.

"It's in the stars!" cheered Grant.

"It's in the cards,"Tica said, and no one probably realized she meant Tarot cards.

Jeremy just stood stoop-shouldered, holding his battered suitcase, and his ratty old teddy bear, Mob.

Kendall and Christina, presuming that they were older and wiser, were the only ones who still had some reservations. They exchanged nervous looks, then shrugged their shoulders and smiled at one another. They had never done something this brave, stupid, dastardly, weird—whatever it was.

As the others gallivanted around the Special Assignments classroom, those two huddled over a legal pad and outlined the pros and cons of going ahead with such a "lamebrain" idea, as Kendall called it. Christina well understood that this meant that he was one hundred percent for it but just needed some coaxing and cajoling to admit it.

"It seems to me," Christina began, turning the lined pad toward her and jotting in the PRO column, "that we got a real assignment, so we have to do something anyway. Of course, we could pick something easier..."

"And legal," added Kendall with a grimace.

Christina ignored him. "...but this space thing is just so current and so important and so..."

Kendall interrupted again, "And so illegal."

"Shut up, Kendall!" Christina finally said, losing patience. "Trust me, I could easily back out of this whole thing. I want to go to college, not jail. This is not the kind of thing my brother and I usually do, you know." She threw down her pencil.

"Yeah, yeah," said Kendall. "You guys are real straight-arrows, I know. But that's not the issue here." He swept the pad around to his side, and to Christina's surprise, began to write under the PRO column. "If we accomplish our goal…"

Now it was Christina's turn to interrupt. "Which IS?"

Kendall ignored her. "If we pull this off, then yes, we either get in major butt-hauling trouble…or we get the great grade of all lifetime and have something that could lead to a college scholarship…which you and your brains-on-steroids brother might already be privy to, but not me and not…"

"Get over yourself, Kendall," said Christina. "The reason *why* we're in this class is because we're *all* smart."

"But you have parents…and money," Kendall groused, blushing at his own honesty and feeling bad about both the blush and the honesty.

Christina licked her lips, a habit from the dry Houston summer, and shook her head. "I'm sorry about your dad, really. But you know, he just may be the, uh, key to our success—if we have any?"

In spite of himself, Kendall grinned. "Yeah, I know things work in weird ways." Then, as if changing thought and attitude entirely, he asked her as eagerly as Grant might have, "Do you think we can pull this off? Great grade? Lights, camera, action?"

Christina smiled and looked down at the pad, which she now spun back around. "Well, we have two items in the PRO column so far. And none under CON, unless you want to…"

Kendall shook his head animatedly. "No," he insisted. "I don't even want to go there, ya know?" He glanced over at the other kids playing kickball with an inflatable globe. "I do worry…"

"Yeah," said Christina, her brow furrowed as she watched them. "I would not want any of them to get, you know, hurt, or scared, or worried. I'm not sure they realize what's at stake here."

For a few moments they watched the barely-younger-than-they-were kids having the kind of innocent fun littler kids might enjoy. Being smart can be a burden, Christina thought to herself. You can't win for losing…you're a nerd if you show your brains and, well, the only word that came to her was *idiot*, if you didn't.

No wonder the five got along so well. Only, she wondered, when did she and Kendall get to be the "old folks" of their gang? She was not ready for that. But with all their parents impossibly, conveniently, but most assuredly (she hoped!) out of the way for two weeks, the weight of being the older, and supposedly more mature, of the kids felt physically smothering. She could see in Kendall's eyes that he felt the same way.

Perhaps it was the long, hot summer that had fried all their brains. She'd noticed it as soon as school started. It just seemed that the teachers and students were cranky and discontented. She knew everyone would settle down soon, maybe as soon as the leaves began to turn or the first football game let them yell all their angst out of their systems. But in the meantime, it was like some back-to-school-but-too-soon curse. She knew the shuttle shutdown and subsequent layoffs lurked in all their minds. The economy was bad, and families would be hurt.

Change, she thought. It's change that's hard. So here they were with way too many changes...and challenges...for the start of school: sudden independence of an extraordinary nature, brains on fire, a project that could make or break their future...but it wasn't really any of those at all, she decided. It wasn't the heat and humidity, or the possible hurricane. It was something that she knew they all felt in their bones or blood, or somewhere, that needed doing—not like a hoax or trick or prank—after all, they couldn't really launch a rocket, but they could take a stand, make a noise, make a difference. Couldn't they? Or, just make fools of themselves? Oh, well, one or the other.

"If Ms. Rodriguez was looking over our shoulder all the time we wouldn't be doing this," Kendall stated.

Christina realized that he was right. Not having at least one adult—just one—to hold them by the shirttails had left way too much freedom and opportunity. Maybe, she thought, it wasn't a rocket they were eager to launch?

Christina was beautiful when she smiled, her "October eyes" as her dad called them, glistened. She stood up, tallest of the kids. Looking back down at Kendall, she asked, "Well, do we have the right stuff?"

Kendall grinned. All of his concerns vanished, leaving his face bright and eager, handsome, too, Christina thought. He ripped the PRO/CON page from the pad, wadded it into a ball, and tossed it into the trashcan. He joined Christina.

"Let's go, you guys!" he ordered. The other kids stopped, inflatable world in midair, and cried, "Where?"

Christina and Kendall folded their arms and took a stance, leaning against each other's shoulder in solidarity.

"Duh!" said Christina, "to the Johnson Space Center, where else?"

Grant, Tica, and Jeremy looked at one another in surprise.

"A'rrrrriiiigggggttt!" cheered Grant, catching the globe and tossing it to Tica.

"I am so outta here!" said Tica, slapping the ball back to him.

Jeremy intercepted the globe with a hard catch and the thing burst into a flurry of blue and green shreds. "Oops!" he said. "Our world has just come to an end."

Kendall looked at Christina and laughed. "Possibly so," he said. "*Probably* so!"

The younger kids led the way out of the classroom in a merry sort of march as if they were headed on some officially approved field trip. Kendall and Christina followed, Christina rattling her car keys nervously from her hand.

11

One thing about kids who have been in a special class for a year or two together, as this group had, and who have worked on cerebral projects for long stints of time, late at night, and over weekends, when they'd also get tired and silly, is that sometimes they could finish each other's thoughts like old married couples.

They did that now. As they headed out of the classroom, each one slowed down to look around at the tables, teacher's desk, and the lab counter. Jeremy was the first to peel off and grab a couple of items from the teacher's desk. "Borrowing," he informed the others as he headed out the door.

Christina nodded and picked up a stack of the ever-present legal pads and stuffed them in her tote bag. As they made their way down the hall toward their lockers, all five sets of eyes were on alert for anything they might need on their "mission," as they had begun to call their assignment.

Kendall wove through the science lab, confiscating a bit of this and that, shoving the items in his oversized backpack. They checked their lockers, peered in a few empty classrooms, and each "borrowed" a curious cache of completely unrelated, and probably unnecessary, items until there was no place left to stash them all. Their backpacks bulged like a geologist's.

The school janitor had let them in early this morning, as he often did. But now they were desperate to leave school before they were spotted. They spied the principal, sipping her morning coffee, heading down the hall toward her office. Like a flock of pelicans the kids swooped in a hard left turn down a different hallway. Once certain she hadn't seen them, they dashed toward the student parking lot.

"Glad I drove today," Christina muttered. She and Grant usually rode the bus, partly because she had to buy her own gas and partly because her car was not all that reliable.

"Of course you drove!" said Kendall. As they stuffed their bookbags and Jeremy's suitcase in the trunk and climbed into the car, Christina groaned. "Another trip down the hateful interstate."

Her brother grasped her shoulder from the back seat. "But Christina, think of where we're going, what we're doing!"

Christina just stared forward as she babied the ignition to life. "Going to perdition, doing the illegal, immoral, illicit, illegitimate, ill-advised, ill…" she muttered.

"What are you grumbling about?" Kendall asked, as he settled into the passenger seat. "You sound like an SAT dictionary stuck on the letter I."

Christina tugged the ornery gearshift into reverse. "Nothing," she said. "Let's just get out of here."

On her way out of the parking lot, Christina pulled up to the school's mailbox to deposit the five envelopes she had prepared earlier that morning. She had forged separate "excuse" notes for each of them, saying that they had the flu. She used different handwriting for each note. She loved type fonts and calligraphy and so the notes looked as real as if their parents had written them.

As she slipped the envelopes into the drop slot, she wasn't sure if it was the letters—or her future—she felt slipping away.

12

Since rush hour was over, the traffic on I-45 was light. In silence, Christina guided the car through the humid haze toward the Johnson Space Center.

She easily retraced her route. Only this time, she quickly pulled all the way around back of the complex, slipped the car through the fence gap, and parked in a box canyon of brick near an empty green garbage dumpster. The car fit perfectly, not sticking out at all, which was good.

For a moment they panicked when Kendall thought he'd forgotten the keys. Since they never knew when he was creating some artificial drama to keep them on their toes or tease them, it was easy to ignore him and wait and see. Sure enough, the key ring was stuffed in his back jeans' pocket.

The sky was quickly clearing to bright sun this Indian summer September morning. Their second visit to the Johnson Space Center felt markedly different from their first. If Carl Crispin had remembered anything at all about the night before, he never let on to his son when he finally got home. If the guys at the Smoke from a Distant Star bar were suspicious, they'd have been on the lookout for "those dang kids," in case they returned. But everything seemed as deserted by daylight as it had last night, thank goodness. Still, the kids were skittish and wary, constantly looking over their shoulders.

Christina felt sure that there was some kind of security, even if they couldn't see it. Still no guard, she wondered, surprised. Maybe he was playing hooky, or out sick? If there were security cameras overhead, she hadn't spied them. Still, she knew that once they went in the building this time, the smartest thing they could do was stay there until they got their project finished. Maybe it wouldn't take long. She hoped not. They'd already lost too much time just arranging, if you could call it that, to be here.

The rattle of the key in the lock caused them all to jump. Tica giggled nervously. When the door opened, they hesitated a moment, realizing this was the real thing, not a ruse, prank, or dare. As if entering a dark airplane hangar, or solitary confinement, or an Argentine cave for a long trek, they each took a quick glance up at the bright sun before they entered the building. The door clanged shut behind them and they moved down the hallway, shoulder to shoulder.

Christina wondered if this was how astronauts felt when they climbed into the shuttle capsule. She'd seen shuttles up close and how tight the quarters were. All that long journey, all that dark space—they probably gave a last nod to the light, too, she thought.

The only sound was their padding footsteps as they waded down the hall—except for the *slap slap slap* of Tica's rhinestone-coated flip-flops.

"Geez, Tica," said Kendall. "I don't think I can take you flopping around these cavernous halls that magnify every sound in those flip-flops. Did you bring any other shoes? Please say yes."

Tica thrust out her lip. "Leave my lucky flops at home, boy? You better hope I wear these and flop your ears off…at least you know it's *me* comin'…"

"As opposed to who?" questioned Grant. "There's no one here but us chickens, as Dad always says."

"Unless the astronaut's still around," said Jeremy softly.

The others whirled around and stared at him.

"What astronaut?" Kendall demanded.

Jeremy was stunned. "You guys didn't…" he began, then stopped. This was very curious and worth thinking over. He was the youngest but he knew when to hold 'em and when to fold 'em. He hadn't spent all his life in foster care for nothing. He shrugged and clammed up.

When Jeremy stopped mid-sentence, Kendall groused, "Get real, Jeremy. We have work to do. We don't have time for noisy shoes or ghost stories. Let's go in the canteen or conference room and make a schedule."

"OH, NOOOOOOOO!" swore Grant, slapping his forehead.

"What?" asked Christina.

Grant shook his head in dismay. "We forgot food, guys. We forgot FOOD!"

Christina laughed. "We sure did," she admitted, feeling pretty stupid. A pantry full of food at home and they hadn't even thought about bringing any, nor a change of clothes.

"Look," she said, "there are plenty of stores out there on the road. When we have to go out, we will. We'll just not go out much and we'll be really careful."

Kendall pursed his lips. "Then that would be after dark, and only one of us at a time."

"Sorta dangerous," said Christina.

"More dangerous to get caught," said Jeremy.

"That's right," Tica agreed. "We need to take maximum precautions. After all, our big project only partly done counts for nada. We can survive without food…"

"Can not," said Grant.

"…or clothes, well—maybe," Tica continued with as pained a look on her face as Grant had over the lack of food. "But we can't survive if we don't get our great go-to-college-on-a big-fat-scholarship grade. So, when in doubt, suck it up and spit it out, ya'll."

"Look," said Christina. "This is the real world. We'll have to eat. For clean clothes, if we need them we can probably find lab coats and NASA tee shirts…"

"And NASA underwear?" Kendall said obnoxiously.

"Astronauts don't wear underwear," Grant shared matter-of-factly.

"Ooooooooo, boy, do too!" insisted Tica, hands to cheeks. "They ain't no nastynauts."

"No!" said Grant, eager to share. "I read this book *Packing for Mars—The Curious Science of Life in the Void*," he intoned dramatically. "The author said they have all this pee and poop gear hooked up to them that takes care of all that stuff while they're flying, you know, zero gravity and all that kinda stuff. But when they're in the capsule in space, they have a potty, only sometimes poop pieces get out and they argue over whose it is. It's so funny...one dude says, 'Mine don't look like that' and the others..."

"You're making this up, right, Grant?" asked his sister.

"No, Christina, it's the gospel science truth. That book is a real hoot. You should hear the part about..." Grant ranted on.

"Uh, no thanks," said Christina. "At least the Johnson Space Center has bathrooms and toilet paper, so we are home free in that department."

"I brought underwear," Jeremy volunteered. He gave a gentle tug of his suitcase handle. The others realized that everything he owned was probably in there, but instead of sounding discouraged, the boy had made this statement with some kind of "I can take care of myself" confidence. With a bemused gaze down the hall, he seemed to dismiss the others, almost as if he didn't care if they had underwear, food, or anything else. They were just irrelevant to his world. Jeremy always seemed to have this instinctual, internal clock of self-protection whether that was thwarting a blow, or being in the right place at the right time.

The others just looked at him and nodded. Since there seemed to be no more to say on the subject of pee, poop, or underwear, they all just waddled down the hall with their heavy backpacks and headed into the conference room.

13

As soon as they sat down, they each grabbed a pad and pen. Kendall found some bottled water in a small fridge and passed them around.

"Hey, look, it says *Smart Water*," Tica noted with a giggle.

"Good thing, because we're gonna need all the smarts we can get," said Christina.

"To do *what* exactly?" Kendall said, and the discussion was at hand.

For quite a while they were all quiet: Grant stared at the ceiling, his head resting on the back of his chair; Kendall laid his head on his folded arms; Tica shook her flip-flops back and forth and no one complained; Jeremy stared off into space; and Christina knew—they had really finally begun.

"Well, we could..." Kendall said, startling them all. He grinned an apology. "We could copy those girls from across the U.S. who got in that program to design a mission to Mars—you know, do it like it was really going to happen."

"Yeah, happen in the 22nd century!" said Grant.

"I agree with Grant," Christina said. "Can't we do something more immediate? After all, that's what got us on this space gig anyway…aggravation that the shuttle program's shut down. And there's no other real space exploration thing in sight."

"We could launch a rocket," Jeremy volunteered yet again in his gentle voice. He always said anything so matter-of-factly that you never knew whether he was sincere, joking, or just brainstorming. Maybe that's why they all tended to take what he said as what he meant, which is what Christina suspected was the truth.

"Right, Jeremy, sure," groused Kendall. "We'll just launch a rocket."

"Maybe we could revive the shuttle program—*on paper*," suggested Tica. "Just because NASA couldn't figure out what to do next doesn't mean we can't. There are plenty of things: new planets exploration, new propulsion systems, resolving the issues of long-term space travel, and gobs more. What think?"

Christina giggled. "I think you sound like a teacher!"

Grant was unimpressed. "It's not rocket science."

"Yes it is!" countered Tica. "It IS rocket science."

"Oh, yeah," said Grant. "I forgot."

"Those are good ideas," said Kendall. "But we should just pick one, I think. Our time will go fast, especially since we've already lost a couple of days just getting here. I think we'll get a better grade doing a bang-up job on one aspect of space than biting off more than we can chew."

"I still like the Mars thing best," said Grant.

The kids stared at him. "But you just busted my chops when I gave that idea," said Kendall.

Grant grinned. "I know, but, geez... *Mars*...what's better than that? Astronomers just found what they think are running springs of water on the planet—you know— that would support life. Besides, we could do a better job than those girls did in that special program, no matter what they did."

Tica and Christina exchanged glances. Should they beat up on Grant, they wondered...slamming girls? Or, on the other hand, he implied that they—these girls—could knock the socks off those other girls, which they believed too, so they let the matter drop. But Grant was watching them, just the same, wary of some come-down-on-his-head reaction.

"We could launch a rocket," Jeremy repeated for the third time.

Before Kendall could jump all over the poor boy, Christina said, "We could, Jeremy…it's not a bad idea, but…"

Kendall interrupted anyway, "But do you see a rocket around here, buddy?" He spread his arms wide. "Do you see one they just left sitting around? Besides, all the shuttles were launched at Cape Canaveral, and I don't think we're going there. I still can't believe we finally got here."

Christina snapped her fingers. "I've got it! What if we do this: Our project title can be RELAUNCH AMERICA'S SPACE PROGRAM. We can design a real launch scenario—there are gobs of new stuff out there NASA was messing with. I've got some serious research saved from a cool website I found. We could at least design the next space rocket and a whole new propulsion system and…"

Now the other kids were excited. "Yes!" cheered Tica with a fist pump. "There's gotta be a library here, and plenty of other reference stuff. We can each pick a specialty and work on it, then combine the whole thing into our report...just like we are real NASAns working on a real NASA project...I can chow down on that."

"I could chow down on almost anything," hinted Grant.

"Don't start, Grant," warned his sister.

"I'll work on the propulsion system," Kendall volunteered. The others nodded, knowing that kind of thing was a real strength with him, especially considering his explosive nature.

"Grant and I can work on the astronaut side of things," said Tica. She was always eager to have Grant for a partner. "Hey, Grant, we can find the..."

"...the Neutral Buoyancy Lab!" inserted Grant. "That will be too cool!"

"This is not fun and games," warned Christina.

"We know, we know," insisted Tica. "But astronauts need new things, too, for surviving long-distance space travel. That's what we'll work on, right, Grant?"

Grant nodded his head eagerly. "Right after we eat," he said and Christina narrowed her eyes at him.

"Then I suggest we start by checking out the JSC…" Christina began.

"So now it's the JSC?" said Kendall with a grin.

"We don't have time to go around saying Johnson Space Center every five minutes," huffed Christina. "Besides," she added, "NASA is a swirl of acronyms: AOD… FOD…NLB…RGO…"

"What are FODs, anyway?" asked Grant. "They sound nasty to me."

"They can be," said Christina. "They are Foreign Object Debris, you know, like pencils, jewelry, badges, clothing— anything that could get loose and get sucked into some engine."

"Wow," said Grant. "I never thought about stuff like that. Guess I'd better watch my Ps and Qs and FODs. My UO, BB, and FOE!"

"What does all that junk mean?" asked Tica, a perplexed frown on her face.

"Those are my acronyms," said Grant.

"UO?" Jeremy inquired.

"Uh-Oh…hope we don't use that one too often," Grant said.

"And BB?" said Tica.

"Boo-boo."

Tica groaned.

"OK, Grant," said Christina, trying to put an end to all this so they could get to work. "Go ahead…tell us what FOE means."

Grant grinned. "Phooey, of course." Now they all groaned.

"Hey, Christina, have you been cheating on us?" teased Kendall, changing the subject. "How'd you learn all those NASA acronyms?"

Christina blushed. "Well, I have been doing some homework on this place," she admitted. "Trust me—everything we need to do a great…uh…" she referred to her notepad, "…RELAUNCH AMERICA'S SPACE PROGRAM project is here. But we need to get settled so we can get started. We're burning daylight, as our dad always says."

"Starlight," Grant corrected her.

As usual, in a group dynamic, everyone has a role. Christina's was always boss. "Kendall, you and I will sneak out and get pizza, then we'll risk a trip to a grocery store tomorrow."

"Can't we just order in?" asked Grant.

"Sure, Grant!" said Kendall. "We'll just tell 'em to bring a large pepperoni on over to the Johnson Space Center where some hungry kids are illegally hanging out."

"I like Hawaiian," was Grant's only reply.

"Tica, you and Grant scout out some sleeping arrangements and where the bathrooms are, that kind of thing, OK?" Christina continued.

"Yeah, cause I gotta go take care of my fluid dynamics!" said Grant, hurrying toward the door.

"Your what, boy?" said Tica.

Grant turned. "I gotta pee!"

Gently, Christina said, "Jeremy?"

"I'll find something to do," said Jeremy.

The others jumped to their duties, leaving Jeremy sitting in the room alone, drumming his fingers on the table. Finally he rose, dragging his suitcase along with him. As he left the room, he switched off the light and whispered, "We could launch a rocket."

14

An hour later, Kendall and Christina returned with pizza, a gallon of milk, and a pile of candy bars. All the kids gathered in the small canteen and began to eat. Grant and Tica told how they'd found a couple of rooms with cots and the His and Hers bathrooms.

"NASAns and NASettes," Grant said.

"Don't start," his sister warned him.

It was good they were settling in, Christina thought. They had a plan now, and tenuous though it might be, they were each comfortable with ambiguity, and she had faith it would all work out. At least they had something to eat and a place to sleep. She wondered if they could even sleep tonight, but she knew they'd be ready to start on the project for real in the morning. It was a relief to see the kids more relaxed, bantering back and forth, laughing.

Suddenly the kids froze.

"What was that?" Grant whispered. "Did you hear that sound?"

"Shhhh…" warned Kendall as he hopped up and switched off the lights.

The kids sat in the dim room in the reddish glow from an EXIT sign as they listened to heavy-booted steps stalk down the hall.

Suddenly the lights switched back on and the kids screamed.

"Wha ya'll doin' in here?" Kendall's father had followed them. "Not allow'd… big trubble…" He staggered into the room, a half-empty whiskey bottle in his hand.

Kendall jumped up and went to him. "Hey, Dad," he said, taking the brown- paper-sack-wrapped bottle from him and setting it in the sink. "It's OK. You don't work here anymore, remember?"

This comment produced a tirade of cuss words from the man. "I do too!" he swore. "I work hard…they need me…"

In a moment, he calmed down and Kendall led him toward the back door. "It's OK, Dad. You go on home and get some rest. You gave us your keys, remember? We'll lock up. Promise."

The other kids at the table sat silently until they heard the back door clang shut.

"Will your dad go home?" asked Grant when Kendall finally returned, head hanging.

He looked up. "No. He'll go back to the bar, always does."

Christina cleared her throat. "Let's get on with our project," she said. "I can't eat any more pizza, anyway."

"My tummy's jumpy now too," Tica admitted, shoving her paper plate away.

Grant pretended to be taken aback. "Tica! You never turn down pizza."

"And you never turn down a chance at a fist sandwich!" said Tica, balling up her hand and waving it in his direction.

At least that lightened the mood. Quickly, they cleaned up and headed back out into the hallway.

"I Googled this while we were eating," said Kendall. He turned his iPad so they could all see it.

"How'd you find that?!" said Tica. "I'd think that was classified information or something."

"Are you a hacker?" Grant asked in admiration.

"We're breaking enough laws as it is," said Christina. "Let's at least keep our criminal acts down to a bare minimum, please."

"Aw, knock it off," said Kendall gruffly. "We all know why we're here. Look, everyone, base your work on the project on this blueprint. It's as good an example as any of a prototype rocket. And here's a Johnson Space Center map I printed out. Both the building and the complex are big and sprawling…pay attention how you get where you're going so you can get back. We don't have time to send out search parties. Let the canteen be our regroup place now and then. There's leftover milk and snacks, and…"

"And it's near the back door for a quick escape…if we need it," added Grant.

"Exactly," said Kendall, taking a glance at the map on his iPad screen. "See ya'll later." He started to head off down a dim hallway.

"Well," said Christina, looking at the map. "There's the Mission Control Center. I'm headed there."

"Leave bread crumbs, sis," her brother suggested, only half kidding.

"Come on, Grant," said Tica. "We'll find our way around this joint with these!" She plucked a couple of flashlights she'd found under a counter from beneath her chair.

"No fair!" said Kendall, glancing back over his shoulder from the doorway.

"Find your own light," said Tica. "Astronauts are always resourceful."

"Then find your own blueprint of this place," snarled Kendall, as he shut down the iPad he held in his hand. Tica shrugged. Kendall was always quarrelsome, so she let it drop.

"Look," said Christina. "Let's just use the rest of today to get our bearings and get started on our parts of the project. We're committed to spending a lot of time here, but let's not waste it."

"Keeping the lights off won't make any difference," said Grant, waving his arms around. "No windows, see! I'll bet it's that way in this whole building. But that's good, then no one can see what we're up to."

"Up to no good," said Tica with a satisfied chuckle.

"That's not true," said Jeremy. "We are up to good, the good that should be done, shoulda been done, and might not ever get done except for us."

"Jeremy," said Christina gently. "Don't take this so seriously. Half of this is fun and half is to do a good project and get a good grade. But don't get your expectations up. We're just a bunch of kids."

But Jeremy wasn't listening. He'd already started off down the hall like a boy with a purpose.

Tica slung her arm through Grant's and tugged him down the hallway in the opposite direction.

Standing there alone, Christina sighed, then wandered down the hallway she thought led to Mission Control. But she felt in control of absolutely nothing.

The National Oceanic and Atmospheric Administration's National Hurricane Center reports that Tropical Storm 10 has reached sustained winds of 74 mph and is now declared a hurricane. Stay tuned to this weather channel for further information...

15

Thoroughly absorbed in exploring, the kids didn't realize how time was flying by. It was like a dream walking freely in semi-darkness through the Johnson Space Center.

As they each picked out a different office with a computer, they realized that they were well inside the building, and as Grant had said, there were no windows, so they freely turned on the lights. It was a little less scary that way, but not by much.

It was not a day for much progress. It was more a time for poking around, looking at the possibilities, and, the limitations. As the kids wandered alone, or together, as they encountered each other down one long hall or another, there was little discussion. Mostly they looked, listened, and stopped now and then to peer in a room, area, at a piece of equipment, or thumb through a manual.

They were timid. It was one thing to have such a grandiose idea for an A+++

project, but even this geeky, ambitious, on-the-fringe bunch was just plain intimidated by the building and complex and what it meant and all that happened here.

"It's like a museum in mothballs," said Grant, when he met up with his sister. He pointed to translucent plastic coverings on a bank of equipment in one lab. "How could they just let all this stuff sit here and grow…grow obsolete?"

"Good word, Grant," said Christina. They had lost the other three kids for a while.

"Adults are weird," Grant said and walked on ahead. When they came to an intersection in the hallway, Grant turned one direction, Christina another.

In spite of the eeriness of it all, the background noise in their brains that they weren't really supposed to be here, and nervousness at the dim, creaking, old building, the kids soon succumbed to the aura of the space center and began to feel at home.

Over the next few hours, the kids wandered the building until they had a pretty good handle on it. They were also eager to explore the other buildings.

"Wow!" "Look at that!" "Wonder what that's for?" and other comments were often offered, and echoed, in the empty corridors.

At first they were hesitant to open closed doors. But soon, they were practically dashing from room to room. But that didn't really end up doing some of them any good.

16

Disgusted, Christina, Grant, and Tica ended up back at the canteen going over the Johnson Space Center map one more time.

"No wonder I can't find Mission Control," grumbled Christina. She pointed to a building on the map. "It's in building 30S." She pointed to another building and laughed. "And, look—here's old Mission Control. Apparently it's now a historic site. Imagine that!"

"My Mission Control is right here!" said Tica, tapping her forehead. "We looked all over this place for where the astronauts train, but now I see it must be over there at the Sonny Carter Training Facility."

Grant looked at his watch. "Well, it's dark. Don't you think it's safe for us to sneak out and get to those buildings?"

Christina shrugged. "It's not really safe to do anything outside, but I don't see that we have a choice."

She scrawled a quick note for Kendall and Jeremy, whom they hadn't seen in hours. Grabbing the ring of keys Kendall had left on the table, they scampered to the back door and out into the darkness.

Moving stealthily from building to building, Grant and Tica had trouble getting their bearings at first. Some buildings just had numbers, not names. Christina had gone to look for number 30S. Grant and Tica were perplexed until they walked out into the open and looked up. When they did, the large Sonny Carter Training Facility was smack in front of them.

"Can't miss that!" said Tica, giggling. The enormous building had its name in big letters on the side.

Before long, they found the door that the key unlocked.

"I can see we are NASA backdoor folks, for sure," said Grant. "Maybe one day I'll get to visit officially and go in the front door."

"This is more fun," Tica insisted.

"Maybe," said Grant, his hand trembling as they pushed open the large, heavy metal service door.

When they heard quick steps approaching from behind them, they turned and were astonished—and somewhat disappointed—to see Kendall and Christina.

"You took my keys!" Kendall grumbled, as the heavy door closed behind them.

"Borrowed," Christina reminded him. She shrugged. "Got lost. Saw Grant and Tica. Tagged along."

"What about Jeremy, where's he?" asked Grant.

Just then there was a faint *tap tap tap* on the metal door. Grant opened the door and let Jeremy come inside.

18

Once inside, they gaped through a large glass viewing window.

"Hey, look!" Grant squealed. "They have a pool!"

Kendall snickered. "That's not a pool. That's the Neutral Buoyancy Lab where they do zero gravity training with the astronauts. One of the places, that is. It's the largest indoor pool of water in the world."

"I always knew I wanted to be an astronaut!" said Grant.

"You are an ASSSSSSS-tronaut, Grant!" teased Tica. "I can't wait to get your butt in that pool and zero-fy you!"

"Just try it!" said Grant, with a grin. He mashed his face against the window and stared at what looked like an Olympics venue. "Wow, what a great swim meet we could have here."

Christina yanked her brother back by his shirtsleeve. "No! We've got to be careful here, guys. If we touch anything, or break anything..."

"The real issue is if anyone can detect that we're here," said Kendall. He pointed to sensors in the corners of the room. It was unclear if they were security devices, air monitor controls, or something else. "Like if we log onto a computer."

"We AREN'T going to log onto any computer!" said Christina. Her face was turning red and she was almost shaking. "We aren't going to DO anything, guys. We just can't!"

Jeremy appeared from the shadows. He moved forward and stood in front of them all. "If we don't touch anything, or do anything, or try anything…we can't do our project," he reminded them. The other kids just stood there, silent and in thought.

"Let's just look and not touch for now," Tica said. She turned and walked off and the other kids followed, Grant last, with a longing look back at the pool.

"I shoulda wore my swimsuit," he muttered under his breath. Jeremy heard him and they exchanged a silent high-five.

19

Leaving the Neutral Buoyancy Lab for the time being, the kids went in search of building 30S.

When they spotted it, Christina ran up and stood before the door.

"MISSION CONTROL," she muttered to herself. The others waited to see what Christina would do. She stood before the door for a long time.

"Well?" said Kendall in a challenging voice.

"Deep subject...don't fall in," said Grant.

"Shut up, Grant," warned Tica.

Jeremy watched Christina's face change. He knew it would. Space—it was irresistible. Like a sickness. Like a disease. Like a desire you couldn't quench. Space fever, he thought. She has space fever. He knew.

"OK," Christina said in a quiet huff, as if getting up her nerve. "OK." She motioned for Kendall to unlock the door. He did and moved back. Christina held on to the doorknob as if this was the entry to a dungeon of torture instead of a room of rows of consoles and computers. "OK. OK," she kept saying.

"A-OK," Grant said, trying to be helpful. Tica punched him in the arm and Grant winced.

With his usual endless patience, Jeremy waited.

At last Christina turned the doorknob and shoved opened the door. The five kids gasped so loudly it sounded like an airlock had been released. For a moment all they could do was stare.

"*Mission Control...*" Kendall said in a hushed voice.

"It's like meeting God or something," said Grant and no one even bothered to shush or tease him.

"Now here's a place with a lot of history," said Jeremy, stepping forward.

"Remember those old black and white television pictures when the Mission Control dudes used to wear those white shirts and skinny black ties?" said Grant.

"They looked like X-Men," said Tica with a giggle.

"They *were* X-Men," said Kendall.

"They were space heroes," Jeremy said.

Christina just stood and stared at the large room with its rows of consoles and computer monitors. Three massive electronic monitors at the front of the room were flanked by an American flag on the left and the NASA flag on the right.

Like some old newsreel, Christina could recall seeing video of a similar room—old Mission Control—during the angst before a launch, the tight-lipped confidence when there was a problem, the blue-eyed heartbreak of a mission gone bad, and the boyish joy when it was *"Touchdown! We have touchdown!"*

"Are you crying, Christina?" Grant asked his sister in a quiet, gentle voice.

Christina sniffed. "No. It's just so awesome, you know."

They knew. They all knew. And it was then that they knew that they would touch stuff, do stuff, try stuff, and get their project done. No matter the consequences…and there *would* be consequences.

The other kids were ready to leave.

"I think I'll just stay here a while," said Christina, fingering a computer keyboard. When she tapped a key, the entire console of monitors came to life and they all stared at the iridescent glow that lit up their faces. Christina sat down and the others moved back out into the hallway and left the building.

20

Back in the Johnson Space Center main building, the other kids snacked on cold pizza, waiting for Christina to return. Kendall listened for a tap on the door. Grant and Tica animatedly discussed all they would do the next day in the Neutral Buoyancy Lab.

Alone and content, Jeremy walked the halls. He peeked in some doors, squinting or nodding, then moved on. Finally he came to an office he'd been unconsciously looking for. He knew the folks who worked here helped plan where the spacecraft would head once it was launched. At the start of the space program, that had been only out and back, like a yo-yo, barely beyond Earth's atmosphere. Next, in near orbit, hugging the Earth. Then later, to the Moon and the International Space Station, and now…to nowhere at all as the shuttle mission was shelved. He trounced into the room and plopped down in a chair.

#

Kendall spent all night in his "office" working on a new kind of rocket propulsion system. At six a.m., he suddenly woke up and was the first to realize that it was morning. He started to dash through the building to gather up the other kids so they could get out of the Johnson Space Center, then he laughed and plopped back down in his chair.

"No one's coming to work!" he reminded himself. "And there's no school for us! And no one is looking for us—not teachers, not parents." He smiled and settled back down to work.

But someone *was* watching. Someone *was* working. Someone *was* looking for them.

22

"Grant, you are the silliest boy I ever met," said Tica. "Can't you be serious for even a minute?" Before dawn, they had left the Johnson Space Center building and headed back over to the Sonny Carter Training Facility.

"Why?" asked Grant, with his goofy grin, causing Tica to laugh yet again.

The kids weren't exactly sure what happened in this building. In addition to the pool, there was some kind of amusement park-looking centrifugal force machine.

"Isn't that what they call the Vomit Comet?" Grant asked. He stuck his arms out and spun around.

"Well, if it is, I sure ain't training you on it, barf boy," said Tica. "I saw what you ate in the canteen this morning. I don't want a face full of that!"

"Then I'll train YOU," said Grant.

"Not me!" squealed Tica. "I'm the trainer...you're the astronaut-in-training. Prepared to wear a diaper?"

Grant blanched. "No way. I'll just hold it, thanks."

Tica shook her head and laughed. "Hey, when we see Jeremy we'll stick him on the Vomit Comet...can you imagine throwing up in zero gravity?" She hesitated. "I think the Vomit Comet is an airplane ride? Oh, well, we'll use this giant cage, whatever it's called. It's sort of like one of those rat treadmills."

"Only this has a death row-looking chair in the middle of it," said Grant. He twisted this way and that trying to figure out just how dizzy it might make Jeremy.

Suddenly they heard a noise and hushed and stood still to listen.

"What was that?" Grant asked, his blue eyes big.

Tica shrugged, her shoulders up to her ears. She looked like she might be the one to need a diaper.

"I think it came from...over...there..." Grant whispered. He tiptoed toward a row of tall cabinets along a wall.

When it became clear that he was going to yank one of the doors open, Tica grabbed his arm. "I wouldn't do that," she hissed. "No tellin' what's in there!"

Grant ignored her and pulled away. He tugged the door open and both kids screamed as an astronaut stared at them. When he fell over—face-first toward them—Grant caught him and laughed as Tica scrambled away.

"Come on back, silly," Grant said. "It's just a spacesuit. I guess this is where they keep them?" He waved his arm at the bank of doors.

"Maybe us jumping around and cutting up made him—it...them—shift and make a noise?" Tica speculated, slowly returning and helping Grant stand the astronaut—the spacesuit—upright.

"He's really big," Grant said with awe.

"It's because the spacesuit's so large," Tica said. "Inside, those astronauts were just little runts, you know. Like you!"

"Ha ha!" said Grant, slamming the door closed, which produced a protracted rumble behind the other doors. "They should put these things on astro-hangers or something."

Tica and Grant took a closer inspection of the suit that had fallen forward. It was an EMU—Extravehicular Mobility Unit—according to a label, used for Apollo 11.

"I guess this stuff is part of the breathing and air pressure doohickey," guessed Grant, fingering the material.

"There must be five hundred parts to this thing!" said Tica, peering down into the neck of the suit. "I'll bet there are fifteen layers to this part alone."

"What are these tube thingamajigs?" asked Grant, reaching his hand up into one of the arms.

"Stop that!" said Tica. "We don't want to ruin a perfectly good used spacesuit. I guess it's what kept them cool in this hot, heavy thing, you reckon?"

"I reckon I'd like to try it on," said Grant, raising his eyebrows to Tica in a question.

"No way," said Tica, trying to stuff the suit back into its cupboard. "It's too big for you anyway. And what if you got in and I couldn't get you back out? Or you put the helmet on and it got stuck? Or..."

"OK, OK," groaned Grant. "I get it. No spacesuit. Not right now, anyway."

One by one, he and Tica opened the doors, then backed away, staring at the row of what did look like real, live astronauts. They could see themselves reflected in the mirrored helmets. They looked small, and scared, in those golden, glimmering reflections.

"I can't take this!" said Tica. "Close 'em back up! What if they start tumbling out? Man, they are heavy. We'll wear ourselves out trying to tuck 'em all back in."

She began to slam the doors shut and Grant joined in. When the last door was closed, they both breathed a big sigh of relief. Only then, there was another noise, and it was *not* from the closed doors.

Back at the Johnson Space Center main building, Kendall had settled down in his version of a propulsion lab. Christina had loaned him some of her research on new methods of getting a rocket into space.

For a long time he read Dagwood-sandwich-thick reports on things like solar sails...*provide low but inexhaustible thrust...* the supersonic de Laval nozzle...and in a big manual he found on a desk:

Since interstellar distances are so great, a tremendous velocity is needed to get the spacecraft to its destination in a reasonable amount of time. This remains a formidable challenge. The purpose of a propulsion system is to change the velocity (v) of a spacecraft, which is easier for small than large or massive spacecraft. Designers must worry about momentum (mv) and the amount of change of momentum called impulse. So the goal of a propulsion method in space is to create an impulse. Rate of change in v is called acceleration; rate of change of mv is called force. You can provide small acceleration over a long time or a large acceleration over a short time. Earth's surface is situated fairly deep in a gravity well; you need a lot of speed to escape it. The ideal propulsion is a continuous acceleration of 1g (humans can tolerate a lot more). Such a system would mean astronauts would be free from all effects of nausea, etc. The Law of Conservation of Momentum means for a rocket to change the mv of the spacecraft, you must change the mv of something else as well. Magnetic fields or light pressure can be used, if reaction mass is available. Rockets need reaction mass and energy…

"And so on and so forth," Kendall muttered aloud to himself. "I understand in theory, but how do you do this?" He was feeling pretty good about trying until he came to a passage that read:

Many of the new concepts for propulsion systems viable for deep-space travel require a new type of physics.

"A new type of physics?" Kendall muttered. "I have to come up with a new type of physics?!" He wondered if NASA had been working on all this newfangled space stuff, and for how long, and how close they were to using any of it.

Kendall felt his forehead and wondered if he had a fever. He didn't feel so good. Maybe it was the late night, or, the idea of a new type of physics—whatever that was. He yawned and stretched. Putting a sticky note to mark where he had left off in the document, Kendall stood up. "I'm going to bed."

24

Christina and Tica decided to pay a brief goodnight visit to the guys. They were comfortable in their quarters, but it seemed so quiet—except for the creaks and groans large buildings seem to emit—that they were on edge.

In the boys' "dorm," a wild party was going strong.

Kendall and Jeremy lay back on their cots and watched Grant do his perpetual show-off thing. The girls giggled as they entered the room and sat on an extra cot to watch.

Grant stood on his cot with a sheet spread behind him like a wide cape. Even though the cot was not a trampoline, he was treating it as such, jumping up and down as he chanted the old *Star Wars* tune:
"DUM DA DUM
DUM DA DA DUM DUM DUM!
DUM DA DUM....DA DAHHHHHHH!!!!!!

DUM DA DUM
DUM DA DA DUM DUM DUM!

DA DA DA DA DA DA DA DA DA DAAAAAAAAAAAAAAA!!!!!!!!"

Then faster and wilder:
"DA DA DA DA-DA-DA-DA…
DA DAHHHHHH DAHHHHHHHH!!!!!
DO DO DO DOOT…DO DO DO DOOT…
DA DAHHHHHHH!!!!!!!!!!!"

Kendall and Jeremy began to make R2-D2 and C-3PO sounds to harass Grant, who was jumping wildly, barely hitting the cot, and pretty much going bonkers out of control. The girls, too, laughed uncontrollably, shouting, "GO GRANT! GO GRANT! GO GRANT!" over and over at the top of their lungs.

Grant's shenanigans were just the comic relief they needed about now, Christina thought. They'd been so stressed about getting their project underway. A good night's sleep, and tomorrow…

Suddenly everyone froze in place. The sheet cape continued to flap then fell limply around Grant's body. No one moved. No one breathed.

A figure had appeared in the doorway. A lean, clean-cut, middle-aged man in khaki pants and a golf-type knit shirt with the NASA emblem on it stood before them. He propped against the doorjamb, one sneakered foot crossed over the other. His arms were folded, revealing tanned muscles. He had a bemused look on his face. His hair was cut so close that he almost appeared bald. He had eyes the color of a Colorado summer sky. His handsome mouth was twisted as if he was deciding whether to laugh…or yell.

Kendall gulped, the room so silent, they all could hear it. "Are you…" he began in a cracked voice then hushed.

"An astronaut?" asked the man casually in a resonant baritone. "Yes."

Christina felt her brain do the Google search thing, winding backwards through her database of memories. Suddenly, she blanched. The astronaut turned to her.

"Are you…" she began, but could not complete the sentence. The piercing blue eyes stared at her. The man gave a quick military salute. And then he gave them the boyish grin he'd always been so famous for.

"I don't believe it!" said Christina. "A real astronaut! You're famous, sir."

The man ducked his head modestly but he was clearly proud to be recognized. It had been a while since he'd commanded a mission. He figured these kids must be real space buffs to even have a clue who he was and what he had done. Some rube had once told him, "All you astronauts look alike!" and it had always stuck in his mind.

By now, the other kids realized who they were actually looking at. There was complete silence, except for Grant's panting breaths.

The astronaut uncrossed his feet and let his arms hang at his side, even as he stood military erect.

"May I inquire," he began gently, yet firmly, "what you kids happen to be doing... *here*...at the Johnson Space Center?"

More silence.

More silence.

More silence.

The astronaut seemed endlessly patient, as if he could wait an eternity for an answer.

Finally Grant did his own fishlike gulping and said, "Sir, we can 'splain."

25

To the kids' surprise, the astronaut entered the room, took a chair, and sat down. He folded one bent leg over the other knee, getting comfortable, as if he had all night.

"Then," he said—he had an uncanny way of looking at them as a group, but as if they each would have to answer for themselves as individuals—"then please do." When the kids just stared at him, gape-mouthed, he added, "Explain, that is."

The kids were too scared to even look at each other or otherwise non-verbally jockey to see who would go first.

Finally, in a quivery voice, Christina began.

After the astronaut had heard her long and elaborate explanation, he nodded, smiled, stood up and stretched, and left the room. Quickly, the kids ran to the door and peeked around the doorframe, only to see the astronaut walk briskly down the hallway and vanish in the dimness.

134

The astronaut says...
In 1958, the National Aeronautics and Space Administration, NASA, was created to oversee all U.S. non-military spaceflights. They also selected America's first astronauts, seven military pilots—the Mercury Seven.

26

The next morning, Kendall went to work in his own private, personal propulsion lab again. He was tired and had a headache. He realized how little he understood all the stuff he had read and gathered, but he was eager and ready to try again.

He spread out his manuals and papers and notepads, called up Google on his monitor, and was ready to start when he heard footsteps behind him and turned to see the astronaut enter the room and sit down.

With relief, Kendall did not hesitate—he turned his own chair around, said "Good morning," and began to ask the astronaut a barrage of questions—for the next eight hours.

Over at Mission Control, Christina worked on her part of the project. She took time to investigate every computer monitor and all the data printed on sheets, tacked to bulletin boards, or mounted on the consoles. She read manuals, procedures, and everything else she could get her hands on. When she got confused or stumped, she made notes of things to look up, then tried to Google NASA websites and see what she could learn.

Christina was especially interested in what the Flight Controller did, and when the CapCom took over. It gave her cold chills to see the labels on the consoles. She sat at the one marked FLIGHT, but read online that three shifts during a launch and mission meant different people served as FLIGHT in their turn, as did other NASA people for the other roles.

She also read that the CapCom only took over after the rocket was launched. This seemed to be tradition. Astronauts only wanted to talk to another astronaut when they were in space, so the CapCom almost always had to be an astronaut. She could understand that. At some point—she didn't recall when—she had taken off her CapCom hat and left it on that console.

All the jobs seemed very serious, important, and, she guessed, nerve-wracking when a countdown was in progress, during the first moments of a flight, and, truly, all the hours or days until the astronauts' safe return. She couldn't quite imagine having such responsibility.

One passage she read in a manual especially intrigued her:

Flight Controllers are responsible for the success of the mission and the lives of the astronauts under their watch. The Flight Controllers' Creed states that you must always be aware that suddenly and unexpectedly you may find yourselves in a role where your performance has ultimate consequences.

Christina did not like to think what "ultimate consequences" were.

28

Back over in the Neutral Buoyancy Lab, Grant and Tica tried to work hard on their part of the project. They figured if astronauts had to fly to deep space, they would need a sort of ultimate spacesuit, so they began to pull apart one of the current suits and see what they could do to "jazz it up," as Tica put it.

"Just quit calling it a costume, Tica," insisted Grant.

As they worked they hoped Jeremy might make an appearance so they could use him for a "new-age astronaut guinea pig," as Grant described it.

Jeremy never did show up, so they finally got tired of waiting and trudged back over to the main Johnson Space Center building.

29

Of all the kids, Jeremy was having the most success. He had found a quiet office and worked on the "where would we go and how would we get there" part of the mission. He never thought about the "who" nor the "when."

30

Later, "back at the ranch," as they began to call the main Johnson Space Center building, they all stood in the hallway and argued fiercely. Perhaps it was the stress, the long days and nights. The disillusionment of what they could and could not do. That they were just kids. That they had bitten off more than they could chew. And, mostly, that they still couldn't agree on what it was they were actually trying to accomplish.

"You KNOW we're not going to space, Jeremy!" hollered Tica. "Quit saying it! You're driving us all crazy!"

"Shut up, Tica," said Kendall. "Who says you're the boss? This is a team effort, remember?"

"I don't care!" said Tica, her lip quivering. "I need a great grade. I need everything I can get. If I don't get a scholarship, I'll never go to college. I don't need you guys messing me up, do you hear me!"

"It's OK, Tica," Grant said. "We understand. It'll be OK."

"Oh, you shut up, too, Grant," said Kendall. "What's it to you, anyway? You and your sister have money."

Christina entered the fray. "Look, Kendall, you're only making things worse. We just need to regroup. Tica, quit blubbering, please. Kendall, stop being so belligerent and definitely don't pick on my brother..."

"Oh, so now it's two against the rest of us, is that how it is?" screamed Kendall.

Just when it seemed that there could be a knock-down drag-out fight, more tears, or worse, the total disintegration of five formerly fast friendships, Jeremy raised his hand to get their attention.

"Guys, you aren't listening to me," he said. "I know our original project was just smoke and mirrors, all good, traditional school stuff about how we could save NASA and how NASA could go to space again. But we could do that back in Ms. Rodriquez's class. We didn't need to break into this place and spend all these long hours just to do that."

The others listened but were still a meltdown away from another rip-roaring argument. Each face was tense with strain. Tear stains streaked Tica's face. Kendall's set jaw involuntarily flinched. Christina gripped her folded arms tight against her middle, fists clenched. Grant had backed away and looked like he might run off. But they all stood there silently.

Finally, Jeremy sighed and said, "I think you'd better follow me."

31

Wordlessly, the other kids followed Jeremy out of the building. They figured he was taking them to his secret workplace and show them what he'd been up to, but he didn't. He took them to building 30S. With nervous glances, they entered the Mission Control room with awe. It was so quiet that they could hear themselves breathe.

Jeremy walked ahead of them and stood against the left wall as if preparing to give a presentation. The other kids stared at him. They were curious, but suspicious.

"The reason why I said we we're going to space is because of this," Jeremy said so softly that they could barely hear him. Holding one hand up for them to remain still, he reached around with his other hand and mashed an almost invisible metal pad inset flush with the wall.

Unbelievably, a large hidden panel opened from the floor to the tall ceiling like a garage door. As the door ascended, each child stared at what was revealed and gasped.

"How did you find it?" Kendall asked in a quiet, amazed voice. The muscles in his neck and face had relaxed. In fact, he looked like he might faint.

Jeremy shrugged. "I just suspected it. Somehow I had an idea that the Johnson Space Center had not been left abandoned. Maybe just closed up for a while. Some folks knew that the shuttle program might come to an end, so I figured that surely they'd actually been working on stuff all along and were close to...to..."

"Being ready?" finished Christina. Her eyes were bright, and though she spoke to Jeremy, her gaze never left what they were all staring at in the secret room.

"Yeah," said Jeremy. "Ready...ready for something new, the next thing, the next generation of space travel. I don't know why this prototype got interrupted or, well, or anything. But I just kept poking around and found this."

"Gee *whizzzzzz*," was all Grant could mutter.

"Golly gee bad words whiz!" added Tica. "But what does it mean?"

The five bug-eyed kids stared at the amazingly unique space rocket poised astride a pair of metal rails. The low-wattage pink security lights caused the silver rocket to glow and appear almost alive in the tremble of air that cooled the room.

"It means NASA was going to space again, maybe soon," said Jeremy. "I guess they had this newfangled shuttle, or whatever they call it, in the works while they still had people and budget."

"Well, it's sure top secret," said Kendall. "Look at how that wall was designed." He ran his hand down one all-but-invisible line. "You'd never suspect those lines were anything but wall seams. That metal pad you pushed just looks like some kind of ventilation thing. Not only must they have worked on this for a long time, but it appears right under each other's noses?"

"Maybe everyone was in on it?" Jeremy speculated.

"But why did they leave it here?" Christina asked. No one had an answer.

"Do you think it's, uh, flyable, I mean ready to fly, I mean…" Grant said, taking a step forward to get a closer look.

Kendall took a step forward as well. "It looks like a one-person vehicle. Like a personal craft, so to speak."

"*Verrrry* futuristic," Tica agreed, a look of awe on her face.

"Well it IS the future, guys," said Jeremy, cocking his eyebrows.

"We could send up a monkey like they used to do," Grant said. He scratched beneath his arms and grunted to make sure they got the picture.

"Or a dog," suggested Tica.

"Or Principal Jones?" said Kendall, and finally there was the relief of giggles.

"Jeremy," Christina said calmly. "We can change our project, but you know, and I know, and we all know that it can't include the launch of this, this spacecraft. You do know that, right?"

Jeremy gave her a look of pure unadulterated innocence. The kind of look you only have when you believe in something and have no doubts. "Why not?" he asked.

Kendall stamped his foot. "Because this looks more like the capsule, not a rocket. No rocket, no propulsion. No propulsion, no go. Besides, we don't know how to launch a spacecraft, goofhead! And we sure don't know anyone who does!"

From behind them, around the corner, sight unseen, came a voice:

"Sure you do."

The National Oceanic and Atmospheric Administration's National Hurricane Center reports that Hurricane Mike, now a Category One, is scheduled to pass over the northwest coast of Cuba at approximately 2:00 p.m. EST. Mike is expected to hit the island with sustained winds of 87 mph and create a storm surge of 10-12 feet. Stay tuned to this weather channel for further information…

32

"Whhhoooo said that?" said Tica, wrapping her sweater tightly around her chest.

"I did," said the same voice. A man stepped forward.

"Dad? DAD?" yelled Kendall. "You scared the you-know-what out of us. Are you drunk? Out of your mind?" But he had never seen his father stand so ramrod straight, or look so calm and confident.

"It's OK, son," said Carl Crispin. "I figured out what you guys were up to that first night...well, soon as I sobered up," he added with a subtle drop of his head.

"How did you know, Mr. Crispin?" asked Grant. He was surprised when the old man—well, he looked much younger all clean-shaven and dressed in neat khakis and a pressed white shirt—laughed.

"It's what I would have done when I was your age," Carl Crispin said. "In fact, over at the Smoke, it's what we all wanted to do *now*, only we didn't have your guts."

150

"Who's *we?*" asked Christina, suspicious.

In answer, another man stepped around the corner. He wore a blue NASA flight suit, the kind you work in. He was younger than Kendall's dad, but not by much, and nice-looking, clean cut. He gave the kids a nod.

"Joe Mast," he said. "Former specialist on this..." he pointed to the spacecraft, "this mission."

"You know how to fly this thing?" Kendall asked eagerly.

Joe Mast shook his head in the negative. "No, but I know how to launch it, or almost. We were on the last leg of the prelaunch activities, when, well, you know: when all that shuttle shutdown stuff happened. I have to admit I've spent my time at the Smoke, crying in my beer. Lot of good that's done!"

"So ya'll are gonna cop-out on us?" Kendall said with a dejected look.

"Yeah, I guess the gig's up," said Grant.

The two men exchanged serious glances with one another, then laughed.

"Heck, no," said Carl Crispin. "We're gonna help you kids!" He pointed to the small spacecraft. "We're gonna launch this sucker then disappear into the woodwork like cockroaches. You can take the heat and the credit. We just want another chance at space—at deep space!"

33

It worried Christina when all the kids—and now, a couple of unanticipated adults—paraded back to their Johnson Space Center base camp. The more, the merrier—*perhaps*—she thought, but would someone soon spot one of them and get suspicious? She didn't want to launch a rocket. She wanted to get their project done and get out of there before they all got in big trouble.

Fortunately, the men had shown up "back at work" with a big sack of sandwiches and a gallon of milk. They all gathered around the canteen table to eat. It didn't take long for the men to catch the kids up on some things. As Christina ate, she began to feel less stressed.

"The Johnson Space Center is NASA's center for *human* spaceflight," explained Carl Crispin. "There are a hundred buildings here, many devoted to spaceflight training, research, and flight control. The U.S. Astronaut Corps is also based here. Of course, we just call it Mission Control," he said fondly, with a wistful look in his eyes.

"Originally it was known as the Manned Spacecraft Center," Carl Crispin continued. "It grew out of the Space Task Group formed soon after NASA was created to coordinate America's manned spaceflight program. In 1973, it was renamed for President Lyndon B. Johnson, who was a proud Texan and helped get the space program started. Of course it was President John F. Kennedy who said we'd put a man on the Moon—and we did! No Roswell-desert-UFO-fake-stuff that was—it was the right stuff at the right time and the real thing." He glared at the kids, as if daring them to challenge him.

Joe Mast took over. "In 1961, the Space Task Group became the Manned Spacecraft Center. Of course, we really didn't open for business until two years later and now..."

Carl Crispin had calmed down, and interrupted. "It was pretty exciting around here when we had the Lunar Receiving Laboratory. That's where we quarantined the astronauts when they returned from the Moon...wanted to be sure they hadn't brought back any alien bacteria or some such from space. Most of the Moon rocks were stored there too, until that idiot boy stole some one time."

The kids were so amazed and enthralled that they forgot to swallow.

34

When the kids finally went to bed later that night, Carl Crispin and Joe Mast seem to have vanished. While the kids figured the men must have gone home, all night they heard strange, unique—and louder—noises than usual somewhere in the building.

"Wonder where they are and what they're up to?" Christina asked at breakfast the next morning. She wondered if they had dreamed the whole thing.

"No telling," said Kendall, clearly put out that his dad hadn't included him in his plans. "I guess we're not invited to their party."

"Well, we have things to do, anyway," said Tica, slurping down the rest of her cereal. "I can't wait around to see if any phantom NASAnauts do my part of the project and make me a good grade. Come on, Grant," she bossed, "let's get to work!"

It seemed to the others that Tica had the best plan; after all, the hours and days were clicking by. As they headed out of the canteen, they spotted Jeremy already far ahead of them and moving rapidly down the hall. He had skipped breakfast completely.

The astronaut says...
In 1962 John Glenn, Jr., became the first American to orbit Earth.

The astronaut says...
In a speech to the U.S. Congress in 1961, President John F. Kennedy said that America would put a man on the Moon before the end of the decade. We did. In 1969, Neil Armstrong became the first person to set foot on the lunar surface.

35

By late afternoon, it was clear that the men were not going to make an appearance anytime soon. The kids were out of food, hungry, and it would be dinnertime soon. There weren't even any MREs left, not that any of the kids wanted one.

It wasn't his turn to make a supply run, but Grant had felt a sort of clammy claustrophobia and wanted some fresh air, so he'd begged his sister to let him take her turn. He reminded her that he was the "go-fer." She was hunkered down over a pile of manuals, anyway. She didn't like Grant going out alone, but so far, so good for all of them, so she'd reluctantly agreed with a "Be back before dark!" warning.

Grant returned to the canteen and grabbed twenty dollars out of their secret NASA cookie jar (a beat-up microwave dish). He let himself out the back door and made a beeline for the fence. He was surprised that the weather was taking such a turn for the worse. Dark, growling clouds loomed overhead. He tried to ignore them, but couldn't ignore that he was homesick, missed school, and especially missed his parents.

Grant hugged the fence line as he ran toward a hole they'd found that allowed them to slip out onto the back service road. He slipped through the slit in the fence that looked like some vehicle had backed into it, tugging his backpack through behind him.

All Grant had on his list was macaroni and cheese and a couple of things from Space Hardware. As he pondered the wrinkled note clutched in his hand, he was suddenly surprised by a large black man in a navy blue security guard suit, a half-a-ham-sized pistol in a holster hanging from his hip.

"What are you doing in there, kid?!" hollered the security man. He was on duty for a corporate building across the street from the Johnson Space Center but had spotted Grant slip through the fence. "You'll get in big trouble. BIG TROUBLE!"

"I...uh..." Grant began, trembling. "We...I mean...uh..."

"Spit it out, boy! What are you up to over there?"

Grant sighed. "We kids, we took over NASA...we're building a rocket...no, I mean the rocket is already built...but we're launching it...pretty soon...soon as I get some, uh," he looked down at his shopping list, "uh, duck tape...know what that is?"

The man slapped his thigh and burst out laughing. "Now that's a tall tale if I ever heard one! Sure, kid, sure! More o' that darn space fever. I think NASA squirts it in the air around Houston to be sure they always got a new crop of candidates for space dingbat school."

He snatched the backpack from Grant's hand and yanked it open. As he poked around the few contents inside, he laughed. "Yeah, you gonna launch that rocket with this-here tube of toothpaste? Then good thing you got mint flavored— that'll do the trick every time." He stuffed the items back in the bag and handed it back to Grant.

The guard glanced up at the threatening clouds. "Don't you realize a hurricane's coming? You get on home now, you hear—skedaddle and don't let me see you around these parts no more!" The guard gave him a big grin, as if this bit of humor had made his day and was going to make for a good story to share with his wife and kids later that night—a crazy local kid playing rocket-man-hooky from school who didn't even know what *duct* tape was.

Grant literally shook as he backed away. "Yes, sir, I promise promise promise—you won't see me again. Goodnight, sir, good..." and he turned and ran down the street. His face wore what looked like the grimace of someone painfully completing a marathon, but really it was a grin. Around the corner, Grant slipped back through another smaller hole they'd made for escape hatch purposes and made a speedy dash back to base camp.

But as soon as the guard vanished around the corner of his building, Grant gritted his teeth and slipped back out. He would not fail his team. On quivering legs, he made a mad dash for the nearest place he could buy something to eat. He knew he would never make it to Space Hardware. They'd just have to survive without "duck" tape.

36

"You what?!" screamed Kendall when Grant returned and relayed his close call. The kids were in the canteen "working a problem" and waiting with serious belly growls for Grant's return.

Kendall was livid. "An *outsider*! You might have just jeopardized the whole program!"

Grant stood there with his head hung, the backpack still hanging from his white-knuckled, clenched fist.

"Hey, Kendall," said Christina, hopping up to defend her brother. "Knock it off! It could have happened to any of us."

Kendall was not satisfied. "But *why* tell the TRUTH, Grant? That was so stupid." He shook his head and plopped back down in his chair.

Grant looked up, face red, near tears. "My mom says always tell the truth."

Kendall just rolled his eyes and groaned, sprawling arms and legs akimbo back in his chair.

"Oh, don't be such a drama queen," grumbled Tica. "I think Grant did good. You don't hear no sirens, do ya? No cops a'bangin' at the door?"

"Oh, don't be a baby," grumbled Kendall. "Just be more careful next time, will you? If we get spotted…well, I think we should only make the rest of our runs after dark." Kendall looked worried and nervous. An *outsider*. This was their worst close call at getting caught so far, he felt.

"Not everything's open after dark," noted Jeremy.

Christina didn't want the argument to escalate. "Go wash up, Grant," she said. "It's OK. We'll eat pretty soon. And I found half a roll of duct tape in a storage bin today, anyway," she added looking at Kendall.

Slowly, Jeremy got up and walked over to Grant. He took the backpack out of his hand. He had to pry Grant's fingers open to do so.

Jeremy stood beside Grant but spoke to the others.

"Grant did exactly what a NASA employee would do. He used ingenuity and imagination to solve a problem. Seems like he also used his integrity. And it worked. Good job, Grant," Jeremy said and gave his weary friend a pat on the back.

Grant gave Jeremy a grateful look and slouched down in the closest chair. Christina gave Jeremy a nod.

"But we ain't NASA employees," Tica reminded everyone. "We are interlopers, unaccompanied minors, usurpers, non-commissioned break-enders..."

"Tica, where do you learn all these words?" Christina said with a chuckle.

Tica crossed her arms and frowned. "I do SAT words. Don't ya'll?"

Jeremy had handed out the paper plates, loaf of bread, jars of extra crunchy peanut butter and grape jelly, napkins, and knives. Four York Peppermint Patties were piled in the center of table. "Dinner's served," he said.

A tear trickled down Grant's face.

"What's wrong?" Christina asked.

Her brother pointed to the candy. "I couldn't find mac and cheese," he apologized. "And the grocery sack got caught on the fence and it made a hole. One of the candy bars must have slid out.

There's not enough to go around. I'm sorry…" And he burst into tears.

Christina hopped up and ran to her brother who was clearly exhausted, embarrassed, and at the end of his adrenaline rope.

"It's OK!" Tica said. "I don't need no calories."

"I don't even like peppermint," swore Jeremy, who'd been the one to request that candy, if Grant could find them.

Christina knew it wasn't about the candy, but she slid one to Grant who shoved it back. If failure was not an option, in NASA parlance, her brother, she knew, felt like such a failure right now. "No mission's ever perfect, but your mission was accomplished and that's what counts," she said gently.

"We can open them all and break them into pieces and share," Jeremy suggested. "I think that's what astronauts in space would do."

Kendall, who had been silent, muttered. "Haven't you read *Lord of the Flies*?" he said to Jeremy. "Or heard about the Donner Party?"

"It's OK," said Grant wearily, shrugging off his sister's arm. "I'm tired. I'm going to bed." He got up and walked out, head hung, muttering to himself. "I didn't know we were sending any ducks to space anyway..."

Christina shook her head in warning, but they couldn't help it—they burst into laughter anyway.

The other kids ate in silence. Cleaned up in silence. Left the room one by one in silence. No one had the heart to eat the candy...then. Later, it would disappear one silver foil package at a time.

The National Oceanic and Atmospheric Administration's National Hurricane Center reports that Hurricane Mike gained power after passing over Cuba and has been upgraded to a Category Two storm, with sustained winds of 112 mph. It is expected to cross over the tip of Florida later today and head into the Gulf of Mexico. Stay tuned to this weather channel for further information...

ᴣꓶ

In the night Grant woke up starving. He sure wished he'd eaten dinner. Something rustled and he reached his hand over and found a Peppermint Patty. It had a note stuck to it. *You did good, bro; sorry—K.* Grant ripped the wrapper open and gobbled down the cool, sweet chocolate mint delicacy. When he finished, he whispered in the darkness. "No sirens, no cops. I did good. Like a real NASAn." He sighed and fell right back to sleep.

38

The next morning, Carl Crispin and Joe Mast were again nowhere to be found, though the kids strongly suspected that they were in the building working hard on something—but what? Still, the kids worried. Had Grant's close call with the security guard scared them back to the Smoke from a Distant Star bar?

After a quick breakfast of mushy cereal, they each went to work. The week was speeding on and the time to finish their project and get back home before their parents returned or teachers missed them was quickly dwindling.

In the lab, the astronaut was waiting for Kendall, who slipped in and took a seat. Kendall couldn't believe how much he, himself, had gotten done yesterday, and apparently, the astronaut must have worked through the night, since he'd clearly expanded on Kendall's premises.

However, when Kendall looked down at some formulas and other indecipherable stuff the astronaut had written, he was back in Stumped Land once more. He turned to look at the astronaut, who instantly began to explain in a low voice.

Kendall tried to be as still and quiet as a mouse. He was flabbergasted that a real live—or whatever—astronaut who'd been to space would spend time with him, explaining things. The astronaut had been low key, droning on and on, but now broached into new, and perhaps, Kendall suspected, Top Secret territory. But he kept talking and Kendall kept trying to put two and two together and learn all he could.

"Yeah, we've been working with rocket scientists around the world for a long time to get to the stuff we need for interplanetary manned missions," the astronaut said. "The law of conservation of momentum means if we change the velocity of the spacecraft, we must change the velocity of something else as well. Magnetic fields or light pressure might be used to accomplish this, if there's a reaction mass available. A rocket needs reaction mass and energy to accelerate. Perhaps solar panel nuclear reactor ions could…"

"You know, this just doesn't seem possible," said Kendall. "I'm sure no scientist, but..."

The astronaut interrupted him. "It *isn't* possible," he agreed. "At least not until now, or not until this rocket proves it."

Kendall gasped. *This* rocket? What could the old guy mean? They hadn't seen a rocket, they'd only seen a measly small capsule.

Christina had been standing in the doorway listening for a long time. Kendall had prayed she wouldn't move and spook the astronaut, but now, she couldn't help herself.

"But what makes it work?" asked Christina softly, moving into the room. She felt like she had clues to a puzzle with not only no answer, but not even any words or numbers to express what she felt she was barely beginning to comprehend.

"It took a new kind of..." the astronaut began, seemingly reluctant to continue. "This is all classified, you know?"

"Who would we tell?" asked Kendall in a smug voice. He spread his arms wide then dropped them slowly to his side.

"Who would believe us?" added Christina with a nervous giggle. "We're school kids." She shrugged and from his smile knew the astronaut understood the fact-of-life that kids often got a bad rap for just how much they knew, could comprehend, and could imagine. She felt he'd been there, endured that.

The astronaut inhaled deeply. "It took a new kind of physics." He exhaled as if a great burden had been released.

Christina and Kendall exchanged stunned looks of disbelief. "But how did you arrive at a new kind of physics?" asked Christina, truly puzzled. She felt she sounded like a teacher.

The astronaut hung his head. Kendall and Christina swapped nervous glances. What was up, they wondered. Was the dude having a nervous breakdown? What was wrong? What was so mysterious? Dangerous? They just couldn't translate his angst and actions—and especially his sudden reticence to share more than odd comments with *them*—the future of NASA. Perhaps he arrived at the same conclusion on his own, because he looked up with a piercing glint in his eyes.

"What the hay," he said, seemingly to himself. "If you guys really want to be of help, don't just push the GO button here…go back to school, study hard—real darn hard—'cause if you want to be NASA and you want NASA to be…if you want deep space…alien life forms…human colonization of Mars and other planets, then be prepared to pick up this gauntlet, this challenge, and figure *this* out!"

He was scaring them to death. They watched his hand as he moved it over the keyboard and opened a screen on the computer. Christina almost wanted to cover her eyes. She and Kendall stared at the monitor, looking and looking. They were in awe.

"What is it?" asked Christina, but she had a funny feeling she knew.

"Is that…dark matter?" asked Kendall.

"A quarter of the universe is made up of dark matter," stated the astronaut, now back in his confident, in-control NASA voice. "And now we know what it is…"

"And, now, so do…we…" Christina said softly.

"*Sheeeeeesh…*" wheezed Kendall.

The astronaut laughed. "Oh, don't get so excited," he teased. "Take a gander at this!" He pressed a few keys and a new screen appeared.

For a long time, Christina and Kendall were silent. They stared. And stared.

Finally Kendall asked, "And *this* would be?"

The astronaut slowly shook his head as he stared at the monitor himself. "The other stuff—that 70% of the universe is made of—dark *energy*. Now, you can get excited."

The astronaut says…

Rockets, in the form of fireworks and weapons, have been around for centuries. The first person to believe they could be used for space travel was Russian schoolteacher Konstantin Tsiolkovsky. He worked out principles of rocketry still used today. Interesting that what began with the goal to destroy evolved into what may save us one day, should we all need to move to space.

174

The astronaut says...
Wernher von Braun was a gifted young German engineer. Under his leadership, the V2 rocket, the first ballistic missile, was created and fired in 1944. While it didn't help Germany win World War II, the rocket's plans were invaluable. After the German rocket scientists, including von Braun, were captured near the end of the war, they and their plans were moved to the United States, giving a boost to America's rocket program.

The astronaut says...
Physicist Robert Goddard was first to launch a liquid-fueled rocket, in 1926. His goal was to build rockets powerful enough to approach the edge of space. FYI: space has no edge.

The astronaut says...
For a long time, NASA's been working on systems for long-term, deep-space flights. A CEV, Crewed Exploration Vehicle, will be three times larger than the Apollo spacecraft. It'll use things like solar panels so it can deploy more power when outside of Earth's atmosphere...a replaceable heat shield...and have new launch vehicles—but that's just to get back to the Moon. For a trip to Mars we might use liquid methane lander engines. Astronauts should be able to manufacture more of this fuel out in space. We've got a lot of new tricks up our sleeves.

39

The astronaut excused himself and left the room. Christina and Kendall continued to stare at the screen, then at one another.

"Well, this sure is a game changer," said Kendall. "The method to accelerate spacecraft today is by forcing a gas from the rear of the rocket at a very high speed through a supersonic de Laval nozzle."

"You read that somewhere, right?" Christina asked with a smile. When Kendall nodded, she added, "Good thing Grant's not here or we'd have to hear jokes about gas outta the rocket's rear end. But this changes all that, right?"

Kendall rocked his head back and forth, thinking. "For interplanetary space travel, the astronaut said a spacecraft must use its engines to leave Earth's orbit. To get to its destination, we currently use short-term trajectory adjustments—burns—so I guess he means...well, I'm not sure what he means."

Christina stretched back in her seat. "Me either, but I suspect that NASA's a lot farther down the road on missions to Mars, and such, than we ever knew, don't you think?"

"I agree with the 'farther down the road' part," said Kendall, "but how far? You heard him mention a rocket."

"But did he mean a theoretical rocket? A plan for a new kind of rocket with a new kind of propulsion and other systems to take into account *that,*" said Christina. She pointed at the image on the computer screen. "Or could he actually mean…"

Kendall snapped his fingers and hopped up. "Mean the rocket Jeremy showed us? That little silver runt of a thing? That's a long shot but it could be! Maybe that's why these guys keep disappearing on us all the time. Maybe they aren't working on a prototype, but a real launch craft?"

"Where are you going?" asked Christina as Kendall headed for the door, clearly in a big hurry.

He called back over his shoulder, "To find them and ask them!"

40

Their school project suddenly took on dramatic new urgency. The kids just wanted a good grade, not to change the world. However...

Throughout the day, the astronaut, Joe Mast, and Carl Crispin now seemed to have reappeared and be everywhere—just not all in the same place at the same time. They made rounds, like doctors on call. If any of the kids got stumped or frustrated on their part of the project, one of the NASA guys magically seemed to appear to help them out, then went on their way to leave the kids to figure out the problem to the next level. They were making some real progress, which was a relief. The week had sped by on warp speed and there was no guarantee, they realized, that they would indeed have the whole week. The weather seemed to be deteriorating, so maybe a hurricane was headed their way. Also, although there was no way for them to know it since they had no television, newspapers, or radio—there was now an All Points Bulletin out for five missing kids.

ALL POINTS BULLETIN!
HOUSTON POLICE DEPARTMENT

BE ADVISED WE ARE ON THE LOOKOUT FOR FIVE CHILDREN WHO MAY HAVE GONE MISSING FROM THEIR HOMES AND SCHOOL. AGES 11-17. 3 BOYS, 2 GIRLS. APPARENTLY TRAVELING TOGETHER.   LAST SEEN IN AN OLDER MODEL MUSTANG HEADED TOWARD INTERSTATE I-45S.

In the Neutral Buoyancy Lab, Grant and Christina were having an animated discussion while Tica was off to the bathroom.

"You can be an astronette," Grant said.

"That's insulting, Grant!" admonished Christina.

Grant looked confused. "I was just trying to be funny, you know, like I always am." He shrugged, apologizing, but he wasn't sure for what.

"Well, it's not funny," his sister said. "Girls and women want to be astronauts, too. Many of them have been, you know. Some have even died in space. To me that pretty much makes each one of them a H E R O."

"Not...uh, *H E R O I N*?" Grant spelled and Christina had to laugh.

She shook her head. "It's *heroine*, Grant, with an 'e', and that word is OK. Oh, I don't know how to explain it. But if *you* don't want to be an astronette, then don't call me, or any other girl, one, please, OK?"

Grant shrugged again. Now he really was confused. Maybe he just had to be older to figure it out, but he knew he didn't want to be an astronette. Mostly, he sort of wanted to go home. He missed his mom and dad, and his bed. He missed school and his friends.

"Do you want to be an astrone...I mean astronaut, Christina?" he asked.

Christina thought about it a minute. "No, I don't think so. I don't know what I want to do yet. Honestly, all I want to do is get our assignment done and go home."

Now they had something they could agree on. Sometimes Grant thought his sister could read his mind. He gave her a slow fist bump, and like always, they pulled their arms back and did some other silly twisty-turvy things Grant had invented.

42

Over in his makeshift jet propulsion lab, Kendall sat trying to resolve some issues brought up by the astronaut, who he'd been unable to find. He was glad to have Jeremy's and Joe Mast's company, but was having a hard time concentrating with him ranting on and on. Sometimes people just know too much, he thought.

"You know those rockets don't blast off by themselves," said Joe Mast, with ire in his voice.

"You mean fuel? They need fuel?" asked Kendall, nervously doodling on his notepad.

"I mean people," Joe Mast added, clearly trying to temper the anger he felt. "People powered the space program. Thousands of people: welders, engineers, trainers, seamstresses, and others, with endless kinds of talent and skills. And it took perseverance and dedication."

"And now they've lost their jobs?" Kendall said, figuring that's where the man was going with this.

"More than that," lamented Joe Mast. "We lost jobs, careers, friends, and the day-to day work that made us happy, let us contribute, made us matter."

"You matter," Jeremy insisted softly. Joe Mast just made a *"hmmmmppphhh!"* sound.

"So the cancellation of the shuttle program meant NASA didn't need so many employees?" Jeremy asked.

"That's right," said Joe Mast. "Pulled the rug right out from under us. All that experience. All that talent. And no place to go for most of us. Space is what we do. The real worry is that all that talent will disperse, retire, move away—and so what if NASA needs them back? Sure, there are new kids coming out of school, but you can't replace all that real world experience we had. You just can't snap your fingers and re-create that, not by a long shot." He sighed and shook his head.

"Real OUT-of-this-world experience," noted Jeremy, who'd been listening intently.

"Exactly," agreed Joe. "Unemployed Rocket Scientist—not much of a pick-up line," he added, mostly to himself. Suddenly he perked up. "Hey, want to see a grown man cry?"

Kendall shuddered. "Uh, not really, Joe, not really."

Joe Mast laughed. "Not me...any guy. Wanna know how to make 'em cry, no matter how big or strong or tough they think they are?"

Jeremy couldn't resist. "How?"

"Take 'em to a shuttle launch!" Joe Mast said with glee. "Works every time. Impossible to watch that sucker streak up into the sky and not weep with pride. You just can't help yourself. No matter how many times you see it."

The astronaut says...
Most propulsion systems rely on pushing against something such as air, water, or the ground. Since space is a vacuum, there is nothing to push against. A rocket works because it pushes against itself, using Isaac Newton's third law of motion: For every action, there is an equal and opposite reaction. On Earth, a firecracker can use oxygen to combust upward. In space, there is no way to combust with air. So, liquid-fueled rockets use chemicals to achieve this goal. Future rockets...hmmm...

43

Kendall's father was the only adult to show up at lunch in the canteen, but all the kids were there. Christina could tell he was fighting the need for a drink. His hands twitched and he was generally antsy. He sat on a stool and made them dizzy steering it left and right, left and right, left and right at a zippy speed over and over and over. He noisily chomped on a big bag of chips.

"I know the launch of STS-135—the last shuttle—isn't the end of NASA," said Carl Crispin. "There'll be a new generation of spaceships."

"Then that's good, isn't it, Dad?" asked Kendall, encouragingly, trying to cheer up his father.

Carl Crispin sagged down and swiped the shaggy brown bangs he'd grown since being laid off. "Would be," he said, "except it looks like private companies—not NASA—are going to take the first crack at space taxis, and such." He said all this in a bah-humbug tone.

185

"What about, uh, is it *Orion*?" Christina asked. "I read NASA is working on a rocket to go much farther into space. That sounds exciting."

Kendall gave Christina a look. But she knew they didn't want to let on that they knew more than they should about any NASA activities.

"You've heard of that?" said Carl Crispin, giving Christina a curious stare that smacked of suspicion. "Not called *Orion* anymore. And who's gonna work on it since they let us all go, that's what I wonder." He spread his arms wide. "Do you see any great new interplanetary rocket underway here, kids—do you?"

The kids exchanged concerned glances. They really didn't want to disagree with or upset the man, who was clearly distressed. One by one they each answered in as small a voice as possible:

"No."

"No, sir."

"Sure don't."

"No."

"No, Mr. Crispin."

"Enough said!" he burst out at them, then stood up, turned on his heel, and left the room.

44

After lunch, Tica returned to the Neutral Buoyancy Lab. The astronaut was sitting there as if he had been waiting for her. There was no one else around. He gave her a smile and motioned for her to sit down across from him.

No matter where she saw him, the astronaut always looked relaxed and comfortable, as if this was his home. Tica was amazed that he would sit and talk with her like she was an adult.

"It's real exciting to see you kids care so much about space, you know," said the astronaut.

"Interested enough to break into the Johnson Space Center!" said Tica with a blush.

"Whatever it takes," the astronaut responded with a grin. Tica thought he was very handsome, even if he was an older astronaut. She wondered how old. And why did it seem he looked much older than the first time she'd seen him?

"But even if we're interested in space careers, what would there be for us to do now?" asked Tica.

The astronaut looked astonished. "Don't worry about that," he said. "This shuttle shutdown is just a blip in a long horizon of space exploration. There are a lot of new spacecraft that need to be built, craft with plenty of margin for the unexpected we're bound to find in space."

"Sounds scaaaarrrry!" Tica said with a little shudder.

The astronaut gave her a big smile. "Sounds fun!"

Tica pursed her lips and rocked her head back and forth in a sort of agreement as the astronaut continued.

"We need you to create spacecraft that are not so specialized, that have room to grow and adapt. Of all the things we've done so far—and that's been a lot—there's a lot more to do, harder, more complex, and it will take wildly creative minds to imagine what we will need in deep space, to colonize another planet..." he rattled on with animated swipes and swishes of his arms and hands as if inventing something right in the air in front of his face.

"Mars?" Tica asked.

He nodded. "Mars, and no telling where else, young lady. We could even finally encounter alien life!"

Tica gasped. It was one thing to see science fiction movies, but another to hear a real astronaut speak of extraterrestrial life. She was speechless, which made the astronaut chuckle.

He rose and stretched, as if his bones were sore. When he regained his full height and straight-backed posture, he gave her a wink and shuffled out of the room.

Tica sat there for a long time, daydreaming of how much she would have to study, and where she might go to college, and how she could get the money. When she finally stirred and looked up at the clock, it reminded her of how fast their time was flying by. She got back to work.

The astronaut says…

NASA's Astrobiology Institute, the NAL, is working to expand the definition of life—on Earth—as well as elsewhere. Microbes on Earth have been found that have replaced phosphorous—typically used as a building block of proteins—with deadly arsenic, a poison. The new assumption is that the search for alien life forms may not be a search for "life" as we know it.

45

The kids knew Carl Crispin snuck outside to smoke quite frequently, but he kept himself hidden in the space between Christina's parked car and the large dumpster.

He'd made "NASA stew" for them that night—"everything left in the fridge before it spoils" and found some frozen corn muffins to go with it. It tasted like a feast to the hungry kids.

After dinner, as the kids cleaned up and discussed the status of their project, they could overhear Carl Crispin and Joe Mast in the hallway. One by one, each kid sat back down at the table to listen.

They enjoyed eavesdropping on Joe and Carl when they "got into it" over space. Actively engaged in eating the rest of the potato chips, the kids tried to chew quietly as the men continued their heated discussion, oblivious to the big ears nearby.

"You gripe about the shuttle shutdown, Carl, and you know it was a workhorse, but its technology is dated," said Joe. "It's not cheap. It's not all that reliable. We need something new. You know it."

"I know we shoulda had more in place before shutting the program down," quarreled Carl. "Not left the space door open for private airlines with names like *Virgin*, for goshsakes. Much less, let the Russians have a chance to move ahead of America again."

"Well, I agree with that," said Joe. "But I'm more worried about when they'll get back to manned flights. Americans want it, but Congress has got to give NASA more money."

"How are we going to get kids like these," Carl thumbed toward the canteen, "interested in space if we don't GO to space, meaning people keep going? We'll lose a whole generation of kids who could be inspired, and not only that, choosing school subjects and college degrees that let them be able to invent the future. Know what I mean?" Carl sounded like he could use a drink.

"Yeah, like we did?" Joe said, but there was no need for an answer. "I trust kids to be interested in space. How could you not be? But they'd better be interested in hard math and complex science if we're gonna get a new generation of manned craft ready to rumble. To do that we'll need a constant pipeline of talent—driven talent, space-crazy talent."

Carl chuckled. "Like us back when?"

Joe sighed. "Like us today? I mean what are we doing here with a bunch of kids pretending we can accomplish anything? Haven't you heard? Congress says it will cost ten billion dollars to launch a new rocket."

"Well, I don't have ten cents, but I still have that space passion. I think these kids do, too. Don't you?" Carl asked. In the next room, the kids exchanged salty high-fives.

Joe was quiet. "I think they're just a little rat pack of nerdy kids who don't know what they want to do."

As the kids hung their heads or grimaced at this statement, Carl added, "Like us, just like us back when we were their ages. And now look at us!"

The man clearly meant talented NASA employees, rocket scientists, and more, but all Joe said was, "Old. Broke. Fired. Drunks."

Suddenly the kids lost their appetites. The two men wandered down the hall, still arguing back and forth.

"Don't worry," Christina said as they cleaned up their mess. "We do have the right stuff. We will do cool things, space things or not. And we won't end up like them." She looked at Kendall.

"How can you be so sure?" Kendall asked with a dejected smirk.

But it was Jeremy who answered. "Because we won't. We just won't." No one argued with him.

ALL POINTS BULLETIN!
HOUSTON POLICE DEPARTMENT

BE ADVISED WE HAVE RECEIVED A TIP FROM A BAYBROOK MALL SHOPPER WHO MAY HAVE SPOTTED THE FIVE SCHOOL CHILDREN WHO WERE PREVIOUSLY REPORTED MISSING. ACCORDING TO THE WITNESS, THE KIDS WERE SEEN IN AN OLDER MODEL MUSTANG DRIVEN BY A TEENAGE GIRL, CAUCASIAN, DARK HAIR. THE WITNESS REPORTED THAT THE CAR WAS IDLING NEAR THE ENTRANCE TO THE MALL AND THE DRIVER APPEARED TO BE UPSET. THE WITNESS FAILED TO GET A LICENSE PLATE NUMBER.

46

The men's voices grew fainter as they wandered down the hallway toward the back door. When they heard the familiar squeak, the kids knew the men had gone outside to smoke.

Quickly, the kids finished their chores. "I guess we're low on the NASA totem pole," Kendall had groused. "We always draw the KP straw."

But as soon as possible, the kids headed to the back door.

Even if risky, the kids felt they just had to get out and get some fresh air. Kendall did a look-around and when all seemed clear, waved the others outside. The night was oddly crisp and clear—but not for long.

They'd been cooped up in the building for so long, it almost seemed like this was a new world to them. They each inhaled deeply the rare, cool Houston night air. For a short while they hung close to the side of the building and kept keen eyes and ears out for trouble.

But the night was just too inviting. Slowly they ventured forth until Grant discovered a stepladder in the concrete courtyard near the fence. The aluminum gleamed mercury silver in the moonlight. Unprompted, he trudged up the steps in the moon boots he still wore from the Neutral Buoyancy Lab. Halfway up the ladder, he paused, holding on with one hand.

Somehow the other kids attuned themselves automatically to what he was doing and grew close in a surprising and tender ad-lib of history. One slow, sloggy, step at a time, Grant brought each foot down the ladder. At last, with great hesitation, as the kids watched, he put his foot on the sandy pavement, grains glistening in the light.

He said it, but the others mouthed along as the tableau continued. "That's one small step for man..." His other foot came down with a bouncy jolt. "...one giant leap for mankind..." And he paused, frozen in a moment that might have produced a chuckle or even guffaws of laughter from his friends, but instead, seemed just a reminder of that long-ago moment that was now history so far in the past that only the future was cure for it.

Christina stepped forward and took her brother by the arm. He looked up in surprise, as if he had been dreaming.

Grant misunderstood her intentions. "Oh, yeah," said Grant, "and womankind, too, of course." Tica giggled.

"Come on," Christina said gently, to them all really. "Let's go back inside. I'll make us some S'mores." She knew that was Grant's favorite.

The others didn't even nod. They just led the way or followed, with one last look up at the night sky and the lonely ladder.

Kendall was last in and let out a deep sigh as he pulled the door snug. It was like climbing back into a capsule after a spacewalk, reluctantly and with dismay. Inside seemed too warm, and even the big hulk of a building too confining. Still, the chocolate Christina had already begun to melt smelled good. He shrugged off the anxiety of encroaching claustrophobia. Although his stomach ached, he headed for the canteen.

The other kids didn't notice that Jeremy had not followed them inside. Since he often went his own way, they just figured he'd gone on to his "office" or his "room," as he called those spaces.

For a long time, Jeremy stood near the back door of the building looking up. Pretty soon, he spotted the astronaut sitting by the corner of a nearby building. Nonchalantly, he sidled over to where the astronaut sat, looking up at the night sky himself.

Without speaking a word, Jeremy sat down in a second rusted metal folding chair. He assumed the same sky-scanning pose. Anyone watching would have smiled at their matching posture: chairs tilted back the same degree…right feet slightly forward for balance…left feet curled around a back chair leg; both had their right elbow propped on a knee and their chin cupped in a hand.

"Sir?" said Jeremy, after a good amount of silence had passed.

"Yes, son?"

"What does it look like from up there?"

"Space?" asked the astronaut.

"No," said Jeremy, "the Earth…when you look back down at it."

The astronaut was quiet for a long time, his head tilted back as he looked upward. When he began to talk it was in a soft, wistful voice.

"It's big, son…and, it's little, too. Glistens like a giant eyeball against the blackness of space beyond it. Looks at you while you look at it. Mystical, magical, like a crystal ball filled with wavy images, or the largest watercolor painting you've ever seen. Rusty red deserts…blue blue oceans… clouds of every flavor—it's something to see, it sure is—won't ever forget it."

The astronaut grew quiet again. Side-by-side, he and Jeremy just continued to stare upward and think their own private thoughts.

48

Back inside, the other kids finished all the S'mores they could stomach and left the rest stacked in a lumpy pyramid.

"I'm headed back to the lab for a little while," Kendall said with a yawn.

"I'm headed to our so-called bedroom," Christina said. "Coming, Tica?"

Tica nodded and yawned. She was not a night owl.

Kendall gave Christina a shy smile and turned one way in the hall, the girls headed in the opposite direction.

"Who's your favorite astronaut, Christina?" Tica asked as she and Christina settled down on their cots. She thought hers was getting more sway back, or at least sway belly, every night.

Christina brushed her long, dark hair and thought about it. "I'd say Sally Ride. She was the first American woman astronaut to go to space. She was good at a lot of stuff— physics, football, tennis, flying. Sort of hard to imagine! Best of all, I like that she got married in jeans! My kind of gal."

Tica frowned. "I don't think I can ever go to space. That capsule is so small...I don't think there are closets...I have never seen a denim spacesuit...no tortillas...no hair straightener thingy...no...oh, never mind!" She flopped back on her cot.

"Well, OKAY!" Christina threw down her brush and rolled on her cot in laughter. Then she sat up and said seriously, "But you could do something else. You really would be good at training astronauts. You'd keep them laughing and comfortable and not act intimidated around them. They'd like that."

Tica blushed. She realized Christina didn't know that all her bluster was to keep people from seeing how shy and intimidated she really was.

"Maybe so," said Tica, flattered that her friend encouraged this opportunity for her, since she really had enjoyed using Grant for an astronaut-to-be kind of guinea pig. But she was embarrassed to admit her desperate interest to find something that suited her that was not a spacesuit.

"But I just can't go to no space!" she insisted even more emphatically. "I'm not wearin' one o' those big boy man suits. Can you see my butt in that—now, really! Tica is stayin' right here on dirty, old Earth! No moon boots for me, ya'll. Ding, dang, dong!"

Christina just rolled her eyes. "Let's go to bed."

Instead, the girls looked up to see the astronaut standing in their doorway.

"Good evening, ladies," he asked in his ever-friendly, calm, assured voice. Christina wondered if he was lonely.

The astronaut stood in the doorway, clearly not planning to stay, just making his nightly rounds, perhaps. Since he was always eager to answer questions, Christina had one for him.

"When did girls—I mean women— ever finally get to be astronauts?" Christina asked.

The astronaut shook his head. "Uh, not NASA's finest hour," he lamented.

When Christina tilted her head at him, curious, he continued.

"Just as NASA launched the first man into space, a group of women underwent secret testing to see if they could become America's first female astronauts. They took the same strenuous tests as the guys, but…" He shook his head in remembrance.

"What happened?" asked Christina, knowing she would not like his answer.

"Oh, they passed," said the astronaut, "but both NASA and the government pooh-poohed the whole idea and dismissed the women. Keep in mind, this was 1961. A couple of years later the Soviet Union launched its first woman into space."

Christina was indignant. She figured that was the era of the stay-at-home housewife, but she knew women had always been able to do as well as men. "So, when did the U.S. grow up and get smart?" she asked, her chin stuck out in challenge.

The astronaut chuckled. "Oh, not for another twenty years, girlie. Took us a while, hey?"

Christina was aggravated. She didn't want to discuss it. She was tired and her head hurt. She had a fleeting thought that she would never let anyone stop her from realizing her dreams—whatever they may be—just because it didn't fit with their image of what a woman could or should do.

The astronaut tipped his hand to his head, said, "Goodnight, sleepy ladies," and turned and silently walked off.

Tica was already snoring.

The astronaut says...

Nineteen women underwent astronaut testing at the Lovelace Foundation in 1961. It was the same testing the Mercury 7 astronauts went through. The thirteen women who passed the tests were top-notch. The Mercury 13, as the women were known, were all crackerjack pilots with lots of experience. They were so determined to become astronauts that some of them sacrificed their jobs, and even their marriages, to compete for a place as an astronaut. Jerrie Cobb had started flying airplanes when she was so small that she had to sit on a perch of pillows to see out of the cockpit. They were all tough cookies. It was a shame the program was abandoned. Disappointed, but undaunted, Jerrie, for example, went on to fly a lifetime of solo missions to the Amazon. Another of the women became a Federal Aviation Agency investigator, and Janey Hart, the oldest at age forty-one (and the mother of eight children!) became a political activist and later helped found the National Organization for Women. *They* had the right stuff... it was the men who failed them back then.

49

The next night they were once more in the canteen having a late night snack. It had been a hard and busy day. Christina knew that they were at the end of their rope, and hopefully, near the end of their project. She figured that if they got all their various parts done tomorrow and put them all together into one package and checked and ready, that they could go home. What they each needed was a shower, clean clothes, a hot meal, twenty-four hours of sleep, and then they'd be ready to greet their returning parents—or Grandma Mimi—and turn in their project.

On the one hand, she was more than ready to go home. On the other, she would sort of miss this place, especially their talks with the NASA men, and most especially, with the astronaut.

"It was sure too bad about *Challenger*," the astronaut said, seeming reluctant to leave them this evening. "And, any of the other space shuttle mission deaths, but that's the price of exploration."

"It was really too bad that a schoolteacher was on that mission," said Christina. "Christa McAuliffe, was that her name?" The astronaut nodded.

"I've seen pictures of the explosion," Jeremy said. "All that pretty blue sky and then this weird-looking smoke. It looked like a big bug with giant white antennae."

"It was a sad day," the astronaut agreed. "An awful lot of excitement, then an awful lot of tears." He stared into space, apparently lost in memories of that fateful morning when that shuttle had exploded just a few moments after launch.

"Is the price of exploration worth it?" asked Kendall.

The astronaut lifted his head and gave them all a stern look. "Ask Columbus...de Gama...de Soto...Amelia Earhart...Admiral Byrd..."

"We get it, we get it," swore Kendall. "One disaster doesn't negate all the success that comes before and after it."

The astronaut nodded. "Good way to express it, young man. You know what the brave lifesavers on the Outer Banks of North Carolina used to say?"

When all the kids shook their heads No he said, "You don't have to come back... you just have to go out. Now that's the spirit!" he added, slapping his leg.

"Did they go to space?" asked Grant, confused at the mixed metaphors.

"No," said Jeremy. "I read about them in a book. They were just folks who lived by the sea back in the 1800s. But when a ship wrecked—and there were a LOT of shipwrecks off the Carolinas in that part of the Atlantic Ocean because there were shoals and storms and no lighthouses— they just went out to save people."

"Brave, weren't they?" noted the astronaut.

"Or stupid?" Kendall volunteered.

"You can't live your life chicken-livered," said Jeremy.

"Can too!" said Tica.

"Look, you could walk over to Taco Bell and get hit by a bus," said Grant, "so you might as well go to space and see what happens."

"Long as I don't get eaten by no extraterrestrial," Tica said, clutching her arms around her shoulders. "Rather get exploded!" She shivered.

"You know what President Ronald Reagan said after the Challenger disaster?" the astronaut asked. He did not wait for an answer, but quoted verbatim: *"The future doesn't belong to the fainthearted; it belongs to the brave."*

"I choose brave," said Kendall.

"Me, too," Christina agreed.

"I choose, uh, sorta, maybe brave... sometimes," admitted Tica.

"Oh, all right, brave I guess," groused Grant.

They all looked at Jeremy. "I think being brave is when you really aren't but you do something that needs to be done anyway."

The astronaut smiled and shooed them all to bed. "Big day tomorrow, rocket to launch."

All the kids except Jeremy laughed at the astronaut's joke.

The astronaut says...
It was January 27, 1967. The three crew members of
Apollo I were sealed inside the command module for
a launch dress rehearsal. A spark caused an electrical
fire and they were all killed, right there on the launch
pad.

The astronaut says...
In 1969, Apollo 11 blasted off from Kennedy Space
Center. Their flight to the Moon was perfect. Of
course, they had a hard time finding a smooth place
to land the LEM, Eagle. Neil Armstrong set it down
in the Sea of Tranquility with less than thirty seconds
of fuel left. I imagine their blood pressure wasn't so
tranquil!

The astronaut says...
After nine successful missions, *Challenger* launched
its tenth on January 28, 1986. 73 seconds after liftoff,
the shuttle exploded and the crew was lost. It was
later determined that an O-ring failure in the right
solid rocket booster caused the explosion. Many
employees had expressed reservations about the
integrity of the O-rings.

The astronaut says...
Apollo 13 never made it to the Moon. An accident
during a routine test left the command module
crippled and leaking oxygen. It was too late to turn

back, so they went on into lunar orbit then swung back for the return trip. Yeah, this was the "Houston, we have a problem" flight. Three crewmen piled into a LEM built for two. Air and power were limited and it took the ground crew to help them figure out some lifesaving solutions, using, as I recall, a toilet paper tube, or something similar? Then the LEM, which was not designed for it, had to set the course to Earth. They finally landed safely. It was April 17, 1970. I'll never forget it. Not the problem. Not the time we had to wait till they came back around from the backside of the Moon. And not the time when they were out of transmission range until…splashdown. You never heard such cheering. Never.

ALL POINTS BULLETIN!
HOUSTON POLICE DEPARTMENT
UPDATE ON FIVE MISSING HOUSTON AREA
SCHOOL KIDS

AN EYEWITNESS HAS REPORTED POSSIBLY
SEEING THESE CHILDREN IN A VEHICLE
BENEATH AN I-45 BYPASS. NO LICENSE
PLATE NUMBER WAS REPORTED NOR
FURTHER DETAILS OBTAINED.

SO

The next morning the kids were up early and at breakfast, still discussing their favorite astronauts.

"I like Guy Bluford," Kendall said, adamantly. "He's a quiet, cool professional. An astronaut's astronaut."

"Yeah," said Grant, "but who is he?"

Kendall blew out an aggravated breath. "He was the first black astronaut. He was the first person to figure out how to calculate the air flow of the Delta wing used on the shuttle."

"Sounds like your kinda guy," Tica agreed.

"Who do you like, Tica?" asked Christina.

"All the cute ones!" said Tica. "What about you, Christina?"

"Hmm," Christina pondered. "I think I'm still making up my mind." She knew who it was, of course, but she just didn't feel like sharing.

"Where's Jeremy?" said Kendall. "That kid is never around anymore."

"I know," said Grant. "He's holed up in his navigation lab, or whatever he calls it, but he won't tell me where it's at…says he's trying to do some program that tells the rocket where to go and how to get there. He keeps throwing around words like trajectory, apogee, effigy? Sounds like a foreign language to me."

"I think you mean apogee," said Kendall. "Apogee is the furthest away an object gets from Earth when it orbits Earth. Perigee is the closest point."

"You learned that in science class?" asked Christina.

"Nah, the Internet," said Kendall. "NASA has some cool sites." He shrugged.

"That's helpful," Christina said, "but it does seem a bit over Jeremy's head."

"Don't be too sure about that," said Kendall. "I suspect Jeremy's smarter than all of us. Besides, I think Joe Mast has taken Jeremy under his wing. They'll come up with something. Whatever it is, it's bound to be a good addition to our final project."

"It seems like we have all bases covered for our project," Christina said. "Propulsion, astronaut training, and navigation or whatever you call the 'how to get from here to there? Grant's on logistics, and I, well maybe I'm the weak link here," she added with a troubled laugh. "I'm working, but I guess my finest hour's supposed to come at launch. Not that we're having a launch, of course, but I'll have all that protocol and paperwork done like the Flight Director is supposed to."

"I'm beginning to wonder," Kendall muttered. "Don't be too sure about that."

Christina frowned, assuming he meant she wouldn't have her part of the project finished in time…but that was not what Kendall meant at all.

The astronaut says…
Guion Bluford, Jr., is a scientist and Vietnam veteran who flew 144 combat missions and won ten Air Force medals. While working on his Ph.D. at Wright-Patterson Air Force Base, he also took military correspondence courses. Before he had completed his degree he was put in charge of 40 engineers. When others went home from work, he stayed late in the lab. He always said everyone in his family was expected to use their talents. I do believe he did!

The National Oceanic and Atmospheric Administration's National Hurricane Center reports that Hurricane Mike has now entered the Gulf of Mexico as a Category Two storm and should come ashore anywhere from Mobile Bay to Galveston Bay within the next 12 hours. This area, including Houston, is under mandatory evacuation orders. Stay tuned to this weather channel for further information...

Christina and Kendall had been working so hard on the project that they were getting tired and cranky. It was clear that Kendall was exhausted and had a nasty cold. The frightening weather was scaring Christina. She wished they had a television. Had there been an evacuation warning? She also constantly worried if anyone was looking for them. She worried about everything these days.

"I wish I knew what Jeremy was working on," grumbled Kendall. "I think it's navigation, trajectory, and such, but really, if he's just messing around, I could sure use his help."

They stood in the hallway near the back door listening to the rain batter the side of the building.

"I know how you feel," said Christina. "I love Grant and Tica, but somehow I feel they are mostly goofing off over there at the Neutral Buoyancy Lab. We need their astronaut training components for our project, but I sure don't want to do my work and theirs."

Kendall huffed. "Well, why don't we just run over and take a little sneak peek and see what they're up to? If they're working, great. If not..."

Christina laughed. "I could use a break, for sure. Let's go!"

Once outside, Kendall and Christina were surprised at how the wind was beginning to whip up. Christina wished she'd thought to bring her dad's NOAA weather radio, much as she hated to listen to that constant monotone drone of the same scary weather warnings over and over and over, not to mention all the hateful static. It never bothered her father or Grant when he'd leave it blaring on the kitchen counter for hours, but it drove her and her mom nuts. She also wished they had some rain gear. "Oh, well," she muttered and chased Kendall through a maze of puddles.

When they got to the Sonny Carter Training Center, they managed to sneak inside without anyone hearing them. They tiptoed up on the stairs of the observation catwalk and immediately saw that their suspicions had been on target.

A shriek filled the room as Tica blew on a whistle.

"OK! The NASA Neutral Buoyancy Lab's First Annual Space Swimathon's final heat is ready to roll!" she cried from one end of the enormous pool.

On the other end of the pool stood Grant and Jeremy, both shivering. Grant wore the boogie-board shorts that he always had stuffed in his backpack. Scrawny little Jeremy wore a pair of dingy gray underwear. He had an orange pouch thing strapped around his shoulders.

Kendall pointed. "He must think that's a life vest."

"It's not?" asked Christina.

"No—it's a urine collection bag!" Kendall said with a laugh.

"SWIMMERS! ON YOUR MARK!" screamed Tica and the boys bent over, arms out. "For the champ-eeeee-on-shiiiip! One length, one chance! Butterfly stroke!" Once more she blew the whistle and the boys dove in.

Grant started off strong. He'd had endless swimming lessons, but the butterfly stroke was a struggle even for him in this long pool. Jeremy, on the other hand, clearly had no idea what the butterfly stroke was. He spent more time flapping his short, skinny arms like wings than he did making any forward progress.

"SWIM! SWIM!! SWIM!!!" hollered Tica, clearly enjoying being coach, referee, scorekeeper, and spectator—anything that would keep her out of a bathing suit.

Kendall hunkered down and laughed behind his cupped hand. "This is crazy!" he said.

"It's not so funny," Christina said, but giggled anyway. "Poor Jeremy might drown."

Just past the halfway mark, Grant peered back over his shoulder and saw his friend struggling. He slowed up and treaded water, giving Jeremy a chance to catch up. Little by little, the dark head bobbed forward like a wet ladybug. When he finally caught up to Grant, Jeremy gave a big grin.

As the boys headed into the homestretch, Tica screamed, "It's neck and neck, swimmer one is ahead…no, swimmer two is…no, one, no, two, no, one, no, two… come on, guys, show me whatcha got!" She blew the screeching whistle one final long blast.

Both boys grabbed for the wall and popped up to see who had won.

"And the winner is…" Tica began.

"JEREMY!" shouted Grant, banging his buddy on his back. He gave Tica a don't-mess-with-me look and she nodded.

"JEEERRRREEEEMMMMY!" Tica cried and the boy, looking like the proverbial drowned rat, gave an exhausted exhale as she pulled him out of the water. When Grant reached out his hand, Tica stuck out her tongue and turned away.

"It's just like I thought," said Kendall. "Goofing off big time! Do you think they've done anything on the project?"

"Shhh!" reminded Christina. "Let's see what they do next. I have no idea but they seem to be having a lot more fun than we are."

Tica had thrown towels to both the boys and beckoned them to the dressing room. As Kendall and Christina waited to see what they were up to, the minutes ticked by as the pool water turned back to smooth glass.

"Just think, Christina," Kendall marveled. "This is where so many astronauts trained to get the feel of weightlessness." He stared into the pool.

Christina shook her head. "Yeah, I forget how much history has taken place here in these buildings. Don't you guess that those astronauts-in-training often gave their trainers a hard time, or pulled some pranks?"

Kendall laughed. "You mean like these clowns we have for project team members?"

Christina smiled. "Just like them, I'll bet. Only for the astronauts-in-training, it was life or—"

Before she could finish her sentence, Tica made a surprising entrance from the dressing room.

"What the heck?" said Kendall.

"AND NOW..." began Tica in her perpetually loud voice which echoed in the cavernous room, "for your PLEASURE, we have the first-ever NASA Spacesuit Fashion Show!"

Kendall sighed and shook his head.

Now it was Christina's turn to laugh. "We gotta see this!"

"First on the catwalk…" she began, and Christina and Kendall were relieved she didn't mean the catwalk they were hiding on, "we have the new Astronaut First Class spacesuit design!"

Very slowly, Grant slogged out from behind the dressing room curtain. In slow motion, he moved forward one belabored step at a time.

"As you can see," said Tica in her fashion show voice, "this entirely new 22nd century design will be all the rage! Observe the fashionista helmet with its fantastic array of celestial stickers…and…hey!" Tica turned tiger. "Hey, Grant, don't turn around! Keep going!"

From inside the helmet, you could barely hear the grumble of protest. Grant flapped his puffy, white arms back and forth across one another in a motion of surrender. As he turned around, the oversized, bulky boots tripped him and he went down, rolling like some kind of giant white beetle.

On his back, he waved his arms and legs in the air for help.

Up on the catwalk, Christina and Kendall laughed so hard that they had to grasp their mouths with their hands to mask the sound.

"Good grief!" said Tica. "Some model you are, Grant! Jeremy, get out here and help me!"

From behind the curtain, Jeremy strode out in the world's smallest NASA "pumpkin suit"—a replica of the orange flight suits worn for launch. He ran over to help Tica pull Grant up from the floor.

Kendall was laughing so hard his nose was running. Tears flowed down Christina's cheeks.

"Jeremy looks like an astronaut that accidentally got washed and put in the clothes dryer!" Kendall howled. "Where did that mini-suit even come from, anyway?"

Christina's sides hurt so much from laughing that she had to hold them. "Didn't you know that Tica's a really good seamstress? That's what her mom did before she got into the cleaning business.

I'll bet Tica just took a real flight suit and scaled it down."

"Waaaayyyyyy down!" said Kendall, looking down at the rolling ball of kids as they tried to get Grant up. "Well, are we ready to go down there and give them heck?" He started to stand up and Christina pulled him back down.

"Aw, come on, Kendall," she begged. "Be a good sport. I think their fun is over and we sure had ours. Let's just sneak out of here and get back to work. We can give them what-for later?"

Kendall let out a big sigh. "Oh, all right. I wouldn't want to rain on this parade, I guess."

Just as Kendall said this, the bottom dropped out and the sound of pouring rain on the metal roof masked their descent from the catwalk and escape out the door—just in time to get drenched themselves.

53

Time was running out. It wasn't just about the project and the deadline. It was that the more people who know about something, the more likely it will get found out. Christina worried that any of the kids might text a friend about the astronaut they'd met, the rumors of a rocket, or something else that might seem innocent, but lead to their whereabouts being figured out.

"Don't even think about it!" she'd warned.

Kendall worried that since his dad and Joe Mast spent so much time at the Smoke from a Distant Star, someone over there might get suspicious when they didn't show up for a few days and come investigating. Also, the more they messed around in the building, the bigger the possibility that a noise, lights, or someone coming or going might tip someone off that they were at the Johnson Space Center. It was just getting riskier all the time. All the kids knew it. So did the men.

In the small conference room, where Christina was putting together the printed parts of their project, Carl Crispin had said, "We need to stay on this thing!"

"I can pick up where I left off," said Joe Mast, looking around. "I don't think it will take much time. I have everything I worked on still embedded in my brain. I just need to be left alone."

Carl Crispin surprised them by saying, "You kids just continue with the final details on what you've been working on. You've been doing a great job."

A real NASA person was complimenting them! The kids could not contain their excitement and shock, which pleased the men immeasurably.

"But how do you know what we've been up to?" asked Tica.

Joe Mast laughed. He looked at Kendall. "You think you're the only one who knows how to hack into computers? Your dad was the expert, of course," he added, thumbing the air toward Mr. Crispin. "I can see the chip didn't fall far from the block!"
In spite of himself, Kendall gave his dad an admiring look. They both blushed.

"Hey," said Grant. "We can start calling you Chip Kendall. Chip Crispin. Sounds real spacey, don't you think? Very astronauty."

But now the men didn't laugh.

Carl Crispin looked at the kids. "One thing," he said, very serious. "One hint of someone figuring out what we're up to— one siren of a cop car...one anything—Joe and I are outta here that instant."

"We were never here—got it?" added Joe Mast.

"You'd abandon us in our hour of need?" Christina asked.

"It's not that, young lady," said Joe Mast. He looked at Carl. "But we have reputations, pensions, families, that kind of thing. We don't want to sully anything about NASA; we just want to help. We have everything to lose, but you kids..." he paused for a long time, "you each have your whole lifetime in front of you. You can weather anything..."

"Except maybe the hurricane that might be coming," quipped Grant as a strong gust of wind wheezed around the building.

Carl Crispin ignored the comment. "You can pull this off...get away with it," he said. "You know what I mean?"

The kids looked at him, then one another. They weren't sure exactly what he meant. It was just a school project, after all: a bunch of paper, a report, right? Confused but afraid to ask questions, they all reluctantly nodded.

Joe Mast cleared his throat. "Space time's a wastin'!" he warned, then turned on his heel and walked off.

The kids were constantly surprised at how often these NASA guys disappeared with no explanation and how fast they walked. When they turned around they saw Carl Crispin headed down the hall, without a word of farewell or a "see you later," at a fast clip. Kendall, Grant, and Tica shrugged and dashed off to their respective tasks.

It was only when everyone had gone that Christina spotted the astronaut about to leave the building. He turned to her and nodded curtly. "Well, are you coming, young lady, or not?"

54

Christina was about to follow him when she heard a sound behind her. It was her brother, scampering back down the hallway. He had a strange look on his face. He just glanced at his sister and kept moving. He ran up to the astronaut and grabbed the man's shirtsleeve.

"Sir?" he said. "I just have to know. Are there ghosts in this big old building? It seems so creepy and we keep hearing, uh, sounds." He stared at the astronaut with his big blue eyes.

To Grant's surprise, the man answered immediately. "Of course there are ghosts here, son. Of course there are. But only good ones." And then he turned and closed the door.

Grant stood motionless for a moment, gave his sister a bug-eyed look, then turned around and hurried to find Tica.

55

There was something different. For endless hours, Christina and the astronaut had been so hard at work that it seemed like time had stood still. The Mission Control Center seemed to hum with their business; it almost seemed as if they could even hear their brains working and their hearts beating fast. But Christina knew that it was just the ever-present groan of the air conditioning system and new sounds as certain computers were booted up.

To her, each new sound seemed to scream, "WE ARE HERE! WE ARE DOING THINGS WE AREN'T SUPPOSED TO BE DOING!" Inside her head, Christina repeated a countering plea, "Please don't find us! Please don't come! Please give us time!"

Perhaps that's why she was the first to notice. The astronaut was gone. He had been there, hunkered over his computer, or moving swiftly and silently around the room, tapping this, checking that, scanning some printout, then back at his console. She could hardly bear the intense look on his face. His determination was so fierce that it frightened her, but it gave her courage, too.

"Christina," he'd say every now and then, as he gave her some task and pointed where to go and said what to do. She'd jump each time, eager to do what she could to help, surprised how much she understood, but welcoming his additional instructions, which he seemed to know she needed just by the look in her eyes or her body language.

It all seemed so normal. She felt like she *was* a NASA employee, a member of a special team, all busy in different places but all contributing to the final outcome of the project. She hoped always to have this feeling. It was invigorating, intoxicating. She felt like an adult. What a joke, she reminded herself, just as her sixth sense realized that this mission was now in jeopardy.

"Sir?" she whispered, knowing she'd get no answer. Louder: "SIR?!" Only the pervasive hum of the room responded.

Could he have gone to the bathroom, she wondered. Had he hurried off to fetch something they needed? But then she recalled the other men's words: *"One thing, one…and we're outta here!"*

Christina grabbed the laminated phone extension list she'd spotted on a nearby desk and punched in a number. She held her breath.

"Propulsion lab, Kendall speaking."

"Kendall! Good! Get down here to Mission Control—ASAP!"

A pause, then in a condescending voice, "Well, yes ma'am, lady boss, your freakin' wish is my…"

"Knock it off, Kendall!" Christina said, and this time it was an order, not a request.

"What's wrong?" Kendall asked, now serious. Of all the kids, Christina was the calmest and most mature. If she was worried, he was worried. But he could sense another element in her voice—and it was not worry, it was fear.

"Is Crispin with you?" she asked, wondering how her mind had skipped right over the words dad or Mister and cut to the typical NASAese of referring to fellow employees by their last names—something she couldn't have known.

Kendall was silent for a moment, but she heard some shuffling around. "No," he answered, surprised. "He was here, just a moment ago. We were discussing…oh, no! Christina, you don't think…"

"Get over here, Kendall," Christina said. "And run by and grab Tica and Grant from the Neutral Buoyancy Lab, will ya?"

"Will do! " Kendall said and hung up. Christina exhaled.

56

When the others finally got over to Mission Control, they tapped on the door. Christina hesitated, then let them in.

"Are you alone?" she asked.

Kendall shoved the door open. "No! We're with each other, what did you think?"

"Did you see anyone else?" Christina asked, ignoring his sarcasm. It was a full time job to keep up with Kendall's moods, she thought.

"We didn't find Mr. Crispin or Joe Mast," Grant said. "Is the astronaut here? Is something wrong, Christina?"

"Tica, see if that door locks," Christina ordered.

They all looked and Tica said, "No, no lock. Didn't think there would be."

"Well, I don't see why not," Christina said crankily. "NASA's known for their fail-safe programs, a backup for everything."

"Well, here's a backup!" said Kendall as he began to shove some heavy metal desks against the door. Grant and Tica ran to help him.

"Not very fail-safe," Christina noted, "but thanks. Only…"

"Only what?" the kids asked her.

"Only where's Jeremy? We just blocked him from getting in here," said Christina.

"We couldn't find him," said Grant. "You know he's always hiding out in his secret lab."

"He'll show up," said Tica. "I'll listen for him and we can shove this stuff back out of the way. You know Jeremy, always wandering around in a fog. Him and his space fever."

"Whatever," Christina said in exasperation. "Just don't let anyone else in."

"Like who?" asked Kendall.

"Not even the astronaut?!" said Grant.

Christina put her hand on her brother's shoulder. "Grant…" she said, looking at them all. "The astronaut is gone. So are Joe Mast and Kendall's dad. I think that can mean only one thing. Something spooked them. Too much of a risk. Maybe they heard or saw something. I don't know how they knew but if the cops or someone was coming for them, then they'll also come for us. Anyway, it's up to us now. We've got to hurry!"

"But we don't know how, Christina," Tica wailed. "We DON'T KNOW HOW!"

"Shhhhhh!" warned Christina. "I think we do. The astronaut said Kendall had downloaded his propulsion program, and it was good." She smiled at Kendall who begrudgingly grinned.

Christina gave them all a sly smile. "Uh, the astronaut and I have been pretty busy here…watch!" She moved to the main computer the astronaut had used and pushed a few keys. Suddenly the right side of the room began to open.

As the enormous hidden doors moved smoothly along a track, like curtains opening onto a stage, an amazing sight was revealed.

"Is that *another* rocket?" asked Grant with a gasp.

"It doesn't look like any space shuttle I've ever seen," said Kendall, awe in his voice, as he stared at the rocket, which was even more sleek, silvery, and much taller than the first rocket Jeremy had discovered.

"HOLY SYRUP!" cried Tica.

"It's a rocket, all right," said Christina. "But not like anything anyone's ever seen before! It's something totally new that NASA has obviously been working on for a long time. I suspect a small, select group of scientists might have invented this—and kept it hush-hush based on the fact that it seems to be hidden right here at the Johnson Space Center—under everyone elses' noses!"

"You mean like my dad?" Kendall asked, his eyes big.

"And Joe Mast, too, I'll bet," said Grant.

For a moment, the kids were silent as the doors gave a soft bump when they fully opened. The rocket stood before them like some high-falutin', newfangled firecracker.

"It's out of this world amazing!" said Grant.

"So it doesn't have to launch from Cape Canaveral?" Kendall asked.

Christina shrugged. "Apparently not."

"Is it a toy?" Tica wondered aloud.

Christina put her hand on the girl's shoulder. "No, Tica," she said. "I think this is the rocket of the future."

In a soft voice Grant asked, "But is it ready to go?"

As if in answer to his question, the rocket suddenly began to rock slightly, as it rolled along a metal track toward another door that opened to the outdoors. Slowly, it moved through the door and onto two narrow concrete pads surrounded by a wall that hid the rocket from outsiders. It stopped just short of a large iron grate.

Grant looked back and forth at the old new rocket and the new new rocket. "It's like Big Boy and Little Boy," he said.

"More like Big Brother and Little Brother," Kendall suggested.

"Or Big Sis and Lil Sis!" Tica insisted.

"Only the small one has a porthole..." pondered Christina, trying to figure out the answer to something that was nagging at the back of her mind.

"This must be Top Secret," whispered Grant.

"Totally classified," added Kendall.

"EYES ONLY!" said Tica, her large brown eyes reflecting the small rocket.

"For gosh sakes, Tica, this is NASA, not the CIA!" grumbled Kendall.

Christina shook her head. "Children!" she muttered, shaking her head in dismay. "Kendall, get on that computer!" She pointed to a workstation to her left.

Tica began to cry.

"Good grief, Tica! What are you crying about now?" said Kendall, as he stared at a computer monitor and tried to make sense of what he was seeing.

"We didn't do nuthin'!" Tica wailed. "Me and Grant just messed around in that lab, in the pool. We won't have contributed anything to this project. Now you and Kendall get to do all the cool stuff while we just stand around watching like little kids. It's not fair!"

"We did something, Tica," Grant reminded her. "We gave Jeremy a spin in that Vomit Comet thing-a-ma-jiggy."

Kendall and Christina turned from their computers and stared at the other kids.

"You did what?!" Christina barked.

Grant shrugged his shoulders and slung his arms around the way he always did when he was in trouble.

"When are you going to learn, Grant? It's not called that," Tica scolded. Then, to the others, "It's a centrifugal something or other. I don't think it's even being used anymore for flight training. We found it in a storage room."

Grant nodded his head up and down. "We figured out how to turn it on. Jeremy wanted to ride it real bad."

"It's that thing that spins you around really fast!" said Kendall. "But Jeremy hates to be sick to his stomach. I mean HATES TO BARF. Always has. I don't get it."

Christina's face turned pale. She shook Tica and Grant by their shoulders and bent over to stare into their eyes. "Surely you didn't leave him in there? Did you? DID YOU?!"

Tica screamed. "Oh, no! We forgot Jeremy! Oh, Grant, we forgot him!"

Now Grant looked like he might bawl. Instead, he grabbed for the largest of the metal desks jammed against the door, but he couldn't budge it. They all began to push and shove.

"We'll get him and be right back!" Grant promised his sister, as he and Tica slipped through the small slit they'd opened in the doorway.

"Run!" Christina said. "RUN!"
She and Kendall exchanged glances and shook their heads. "Kids!" Kendall said.

Christina nodded, then turned back to her computer monitor. The first rocket was now in position. While they'd been dealing with "the kids," the metal grate in the center of the concrete pad beneath the rocket had opened.

"Oh," said Kendall, "now I see how they're working this. Christina…" he began then stopped. As an overhead panel separating the two rockets suddenly began to yawn open, he added, "Oh, no I don't see…"

They both stared as a robotic arm lifted the smaller, fatter rocket up, over, and onto the top of the taller, narrower rocket. With only a slight quiver and almost no sound, the nose cone snuggly moved into place. Now the two so-called rockets, appeared as a single magnificent spacecraft.

"Well take a look at that!" Kendall marveled.

As if this magic was not enough, the nose cone began to spin slowly until what was apparently the front of it faced them. It looked the same, except for a small porthole window, its pane flickering with reflected light.

"This is really creepy," swore Christina. "I feel as if unseen hands are guiding this thing. You and I might as well sit back and relax?" she wondered aloud, fascinated by all that had happened before their eyes.

But this was only the beginning.

58

Suddenly, Christina gasped as she and Kendall watched the array of computers and their monitors begin to operate on their own...it was clear that a pre-programmed software program was initiating liftoff procedures.

"But we're not ready..." said Christina. "We're not ready!"

Kendall shook his head. "No, *we're* not ready." He pointed to the spacecraft. But *it* is."

Just then, a strong wind sloshed over the roof. They had no idea if the hurricane was coming, upon them, skirting the area, or what.

"I think our weather window is closing, too," Kendall guessed. At least the pelting rain they'd heard earlier had stopped. Stars and a sliver of Moon hovered overhead like a planetarium dome.

"Surely this is not the eye of the hurricane?" Christina mumbled, mostly to herself.

Suddenly, enormous monitors on each side of the open bay doors came on, twin images showing the spacecraft and a small spit of steam as the propulsion system began to ignite.

The National Oceanic and Atmospheric Administration's National Hurricane Center reports that Hurricane Mike became a Category Three storm as it approached the Texas coast. As it hit land, wind speeds dropped, downgrading it to a Category Two storm as it heads over the Houston area. Please heed all warnings and evacuation notices, and stay tuned to this weather channel for further information...

ALL POINTS BULLETIN!
HOUSTON POLICE DEPARTMENT

BE ON THE LOOKOUT: OLDER MODEL
MUSTANG, LICENSE PLATE UNKNOWN;
LAST SEEN NASA 1, BYPASS E. POSSIBLE
FIVE MISSING SCHOOL KIDS. DESTINATION
UNKNOWN. APPARENTLY 3 BOYS, 2 GIRLS;
PROBABLE ALL TEENS. IN NO APPARENT
DANGER. NAMES UNKNOWN. PLEASE
ADVISE ANY SIGHTINGS, INFO TO HPD.

59

Grant and Tica raced back to the Sonny Carter Training Facility where they had reluctantly allowed Jeremy to get in the retired "spin cycle machine," as Grant called it. A few hours ago they'd revved up the machine and let Jeremy have a go at zero gravity. They'd run back to the Neutral Buoyancy Lab to get something, and somehow ("Like a couple of dang dorks!" Tica now said) forgotten their friend.

Once inside the building, they ran so fast that they skidded on the slick floors right past the entrance to the large storage area where they'd left their friend in slingshot mode aboard an obsolete monster of a trainer.

"Hurry, Grant!" Tica shouted, scuttling like a crab back to the doorway. "Every second counts!"

In a frantic cry, Grant combined "Where are you?" and "Jeremy!" into one desperate plea as he bounded into the room. "WHEREMY?! WHEREMY?!"

"He's not here!" screamed Tica.

They stopped cold when they saw that the machine they'd left Jeremy in had stopped. There was no sign of Jeremy, nor of gobs of vomit, much to Grant's relief.

As they turned to leave, Tica spotted a note taped to the back of the door they had just entered. *Gone to the Flight Simulation Lab and some other places. See you later.—J*

"Now why would he go there?" asked Tica.

"Cause it's fun," said Grant. "It's like some cool, virtual video game. And I'll bet he didn't go there...I'll bet he *staggered* there!" Grant staggered back and forth across the room.

"Well, I wish he'd left a trail of dang breadcrumbs," said Tica, looking left and right.

"Or barf balls!" said Grant.

"Oh, come on," said Tica, rolling her eyes. "Let's go back to Mission Control and see if he showed up there. Hey..."

For a moment both kids stood stark still, arms akimbo, listening. A subdued roaring could be felt more than heard.

"What's that?" asked Grant.

"The rocket?" guessed Tica, eyes wide. "Or the hurricane?!"

"It better NOT be the rocket!" shouted Grant. "Come, on, Tica! We don't want to miss the launch!"

60

Back at Mission Control, Kendall and Christina stared in fear at the powerful burn beneath the rocket. As they watched they felt the same as all NASA workers—from the janitor to the top scientists to the astronauts themselves—that hold your breath, oh my gosh, this is really gonna happen feeling.

But it wasn't going to happen.

"What's wrong, Kendall?" Christina asked. There was a desperate urgency in her voice. "Everything seems to be on hold."

"I know, I know!" said Kendall, staring at his monitor, afraid to push any key. "What do you see on your monitor?"

Christina didn't answer. She appeared to be lost in thought. Kendall was shocked to see a look of failure appear in Christina's downturned eyes and mouth.

"What's wrong, Christina? What's wrong?!" Kendall pleaded.

Suddenly there was a racket behind them as Tica and Grant burst into the room.

"Did we miss it?! Did we miss it?!" Grant squealed.

"Don't be stupid, Grant," said Tica. "There it sits! Hey, so why is it just sitting there? Why isn't it going anywhere? And, by the way," she asked, looking back and forth, "did the two rockets mate, or what?!"

Christina motioned for them all to gather around her. "Look!"

As they stared over her shoulder at her computer monitor, they read:

LAUNCH SEQUENCE COMPLETE...
PROPULSION AT MAX HOLD....
HOLDING FOR LAUNCH KEY...
HOLDING FOR LAUNCH KEY...
HOLDING FOR LAUNCH KEY...

The words mesmerized them. The words flashed on and off, as if begging for an answer. The T-Minus clock was frozen at T-Minus One.

"Oh, my gosh," said Kendall. "What are we going to do? The program won't continue without a launch key!"

"Well, we don't have a launch key!" said Christina. "Why didn't the astronaut tell me before he left? Why? Why?!"

"I guess he was in a hurry," said Tica softly, tears beginning to well in her eyes.

"NO!" cried Kendall. "You said it, Christina. NASA always has a fail-safe! He just wouldn't have left us without a way to launch this thing. It must be here! It has to be here. Look for it! Fast—or we'll run out of propulsion and this launch will fizzle right in front of our eyes!"

Desperate, all the kids stared at everything in the room. They ran from workstation to workstation, peered at every monitor, every notepad, but they saw nothing that looked like a launch key.

"I don't see no dang key!" shouted Tica.

Christina looked up and said, "Hey, you guys, you DO know we're not looking for a key, don't you?"

"Key…ignition…liftoff…" said Grant, puzzled.

"A launch key is a *code!*" shouted Christina. "A sequence of numbers or numbers and letters."

Kendall laughed maniacally, the feeling of failure—when failure was not an option—beginning to gnaw at his gut. "Well, there are a million numbers in this joint! A gazillion! A nanonillion!..."

"Listen!" Tica cried in a voice that made them all hush.

"Someone's coming!" said Kendall. "That's the sound of that darn metal fence gate." They could also hear distant sirens. Then he looked at the rocket. "That propulsion won't hold forever, Christina."

"I know," Christina answered. She was not thinking about the rocket or the fire beneath it or the sound of people headed their way. She was thinking about the astronaut. His calmness. His determination. His intensity. She knew that he wanted this spacecraft to launch. "We're just kids," she muttered, "just kids. He knew that."

"Yeah," said Grant, now in tune to his sister's thinking. "So what do you do when you want a kid to remember something you're afraid they'll forget, like their home phone number, or their street address, or..."

Christina snapped her fingers. "That's it! That's it, Grant! Something simple. Something even a kid wouldn't forget! Something as simple and silly as SESAME STREET!"

"Huh?" the other kids said. The gate was rattling louder now. They could hear shouting and more sirens, even the whir of helicopter blades.

"Like this program is brought to you by the letter A?" guessed Grant.

Christina surprised them all by laughing. How often, she thought, had she heard the astronaut hum that old rock and roll song? Quickly, but calmly, she pushed the letters ABC and then the numbers 123. They held their breaths. "ABC...Easy as 123..." she chirped.

LAUNCH KEY ACCEPTED...
IGNITION UNDERWAY...
PRESS GO FOR LAUNCH...
PRESS GO FOR LAUNCH...
PRESS GO FOR LAUNCH...

"I always wanted to do this!" squealed Tica, hopping into the seat designated for the PAO, Public Affairs Officer. As the angst and technology and rumble continued with the rocket launch, she launched into her own tirade.

She leaned into a microphone set up on the console. "Hi, ya'll, listenin' out there in non-space land, better known as Earth, this is Tica, uh, Tica Talker, your, your, as it says here, PAO officer. Now that is not a Chinese take-out dish, that is, I am 'The Voice of Mission Control.' So listen up, cause we're about to launch a rocket here, folks!"

The other kids were too busy to laugh at Tica's fake broadcast.

Almost instantaneously, Tica was flustered when she began to hear strange voices in her ear. As she pushed at buttons on the computer to make them stop, she instead hit the OPEN MIC button and everyone in the room heard:

This is Baikonur Cosmodrome...this is Mission Control Center in Korolyov, Russia... European Space Operations Centre, Germany here...what is up?... please advise have we missed something, Houston?...Guiana Space Center seeking detail of imminent launch, Houston, please advise...Tanegashima Space Center asks if data transmission received Houston is accurate...Tsukuba Space Center, Japan...Houston...please advise immediately...

"Tica!" hollered Kendall. "What have you done?" He scrambled back to her console, took a look, and gasped. "You hit the transmit button! You've been broadcasting live—to the world!"

As the barrage of global inquiries continued to pour in, Tica grew pale and quiet. Kendall ran back to his workstation. "Can't worry about that now," he said to Christina, who also looked pale for a variety of reasons. "But this cat is outta the bag. We are so in trouble."

In the background, they could hear a tremulous voice as Tica tried to fix things. "Uh, ya'll out there. I can explain. We are just playing around here. I mean I am just making up this junk…I'm just a kid…do not listen to me…pay no mind to the silly stuff you just heard me say…I promise…"

Without even turning around, Christina and Kendall called back together, "TICA…HUSH!"

But their problems were growing. The T-Minus clock shut down again. The kids were stunned.

"What now?" grumbled Kendall.

Christina stared at the monitors and the rocket. "Look!" she said. "The rocket didn't get all the way out on the track." She pointed to the rail that extended outside of the building.

"How did we miss that?" said Kendall. "Of course! If the rocket went off where it's standing, it would blast right through part of the roof."

"Yeah," said Grant, moving close—too close—to peer at the track. "The rocket has to get out there under clear sky, and, right over that grate thing, I think."

"But how?" asked Christina, once more staring at buttons and levers, and wondering...when suddenly, the spacecraft gave a frightening left-tilt/right-tilt shudder and began to move forward again.

"Yaaaayyyyyyyyyyyy!" the kids cheered, relieved that the rocket had overcome the problem on its own."

Christina and Kendall exchanged embarrassed glances. "That, uh, wasn't very NASAlike," said Kendall.

"Aw, I've seen them cheer on the NASA TV channel," said Christina. "And now I know why!"

"It's now or never, Christina," Kendall said with surprising gentleness. Even over the wind, they could hear sirens growing ever closer. Lightning flashed on the horizon, but directly overhead they could see stars and the Moon. The eye of the hurricane was directly overhead.

ALL POINTS BULLETIN!!!
HOUSTON POLICE DEPARTMENT

BE ADVISED WE NOW HAVE NAMES, AGES, PHOTOS ON HPD WEBSITE FOR FIVE MISSING AREA SCHOOL KIDS. LAST SEEN IN CLEARWATER AREA. BE ON LOOKOUT. POSSIBLY DRIVING LATE MODEL MUSTANG.

62

They all stared at the rocket and seemed to have a hard time thinking of what to say or do. "Christina?" Kendall repeated. He nudged her.

Christina sat at the console labeled FLIGHT and stared up at the sky. "I always thought it would be different," she said softly, to no one. "I thought I'd be a real flight director...at a desk...watching a monitor of a rocket somewhere else...not virtually outside in a concrete bunker that stinks of dumpster garbage." She sighed. "Oh, well—I guess this is real life, not Hollywood."

For a moment there was silence; not even the frogs in a nearby pond dared croak.

Suddenly, once more, the automatic launch sequence picked up where it had left off until finally the rocket lurched into its final correct place and shuddered to a stop. At that time, the monitor returned to its HOLDING FOR LAUNCH CODE mode and the kids groaned.

Of course, this time Christina knew what to do.

There was a moment of silence as they all just stared at the screen. Then another monitor *bleeped bleeped bleeped* a warning:

AUTOMATIC ABORT MODE IN 20 SECONDS...
AUTOMATIC ABORT MODE IN 20 SECONDS...
LAUNCH SEQUENCE REQUIRES GO FOR LAUNCH CONCENSUS...LAUNCH SEQUENCE...

They just couldn't scrub this mission, she thought. Taking charge, Christina polled the others. Each stared intently at their respective monitors, which showed no apparent problems or issues.

"Are you GO or NO GO for launch?" demanded Christina, sitting in the front row "trench" at the console designated FLIGHT.

"GUIDANCE is go for launch!" said Tica.

"GNC is GO for launch!" cried Grant in a trembling voice.

They all held their breaths.

"PROP is GO for launch!" Kendall said and they all waited.

And waited.

And waited on Christina.

"Are we go for launch, FLIGHT?" demanded the astronaut's voice that Christina could hear in her mind. "FLIGHT?" he repeated in an urgent and stern voice. It was not a question. It was a demand for an answer—now. The auto-abort was five seconds away from activating, as they could all clearly see from the flashing monitor.

Christina flinched. This was no longer a school assignment. This was the real thing. For the first time, based on what they had seen when the astronaut showed them the dark matter and new type of physics data, she realized launching an entirely new type of rocket was indeed possible. *Possible*, but untried.

Kendall quickly jumped up from in front of his computer. He moved to Christina's side. "We are *all systems go*, Christina," he reminded her with a whisper in her ear.

Christina sat down gently. Her front teeth sunk into her bottom lip. She nodded several times at her monitor as she rechecked data one last time. It was no time for a mistake. Finally, with confidence, she said in a firm and loud voice: "FLIGHT is GO for launch!" And then she pushed the button that set the launch in motion.

64

As soon as the countdown clock restarted, Christina felt the power of what was beginning to happen. The floor, their seats, the room seemed to rumble and vibrate so hard that she felt they, too, would lift off with the rocket.

"Wow!" she heard her brother say, "I think the throttle's up my butt," and she knew he felt the same eerie "leaving Earth" sensation.

ALL POINTS BULLETIN!
HOUSTON POLICE DEPARTMENT

IMMEDIATE NOTICE! ONE OF THE FIVE MISSING HOUSTON KIDS SEEN IN THE VICINITY OF THE JOHNSON SPACE CENTER. THESE CHILDREN HAVE POSSIBLY BREACHED JSC SECURITY. MAY BE ARMED AND DANGEROUS. PURPOSES UNKNOWN. ACCOMPLICES UNKNOWN. EXERT CAUTION. COORDINATE ALL EFFORTS THRU HPD AND NASA SECURITY.

65

"TEN!…" cried Kendall. The word was barely audible in the room now alive with noise from within and without. The rocket seemed to inhale.

"NINE…" said Grant and the scent of smoke streamed beneath his nose.

"EIGHT…" said Tica with a nervous giggle.

A silent blast of ghostly white smoke shot out from under the main engine.

Next, a neon Halloween orange light cushioned the rocket. Waves of heat flowed toward the Mission Control room.

"We should move back!" said Kendall. "SEVEN."

"Where to?" Christina said.

The rocket tottered slightly, then straightened. The burgeoning flames dimmed somewhat then burst forth more vibrantly. A powerful hiss emanated from the exciting, yet frightening thing before them.

"SIX…" Tica and Grant said together.

"Hey, where is Jeremy?" Christina asked suddenly. There was a hint of panic in her voice. She looked all around. "He wouldn't want to miss this!"

"FIVE!" said Kendall. His face was covered in sweat in spite of the cool night air billowing over them.

"Did you hear me?!" shouted Christina over the increasing roar of the engine. "Didn't you bring him back with you?!"

"FOUR!" was the only answer from the other three kids.

"Jeremy? JEREMY?!" Christina hollered.

She looked up at the rocket. A pain shot across her chest, and she screamed.

66

"Jeremy! Jeremy! What are you doing?!" screamed Christina. She thrust her arm at the quivering rocket. Through the spiraling condensation they could see...

"JEREMY!!!!!!" they all cried together.

His small, pale face hovered in the center of porthole. Looking little and frail in the tattered white tee shirt beneath his orange "fashion show" flight suit, Jeremy ducked his head in a kind of apology.

"THHHREEEEEE!"

"NOOO!!!!!" screamed Christina. She stretched out her hands as if she could reach forth and pluck the boy from the spacecraft.

"Kendall, is there a kill switch, an abort button?" Christina cried. "We've got to get him out of there NOW!"

Kendall scrambled to look for one.

Ignition was imminent. Christina glanced at the monitor and said in as controlled a voice as she could manage, "Jeremy...we have to know...we have to know now...NOW, Jeremy, now!"

Four kids stared with bug-eyes at their friend who gave them a thumbs-up A-OK sign. But Christina was not satisfied with that.

"Kendall, find that ABORT MISSION button!" Christina yelled. In her peripheral vision—her eyes were glued to Jeremy's eyes—she saw Kendall's hand move.

Jeremy shook his head again, slowly. He smiled.

Grant gasped. "Look, Christina!" he said, tugging at the sleeve of her lab coat. "It's OK. He smiled. Jeremy smiled!"

Tears flowed down Christina's cheeks as Jeremy raised his right hand and mashed it into the small window of the capsule.

"He wants out," she whispered.

"No!" Grant said sternly. "Look! He's giving us a high-five."

One by one the kids slowly raised their hands up and toward their friend.

With a shy look, Jeremy lifted something up for them to see. It was his teddy bear, the one they always teased him about.

"It's Mob," said Tica softly.

"TWO!" Kendall hollered at the top of his lungs.

The rocket tottered, then straightened. Flames dimmed then burst forth more vibrantly. A powerful, all-consuming hiss filled their ears. Power of a caliber never before witnessed rocked the building. Involuntarily, they all stepped backwards as the heat and concussion of energy slapped and grabbed at them.

Grant leaned against the back wall, hands on his hips, elbows thrust out, eyes big, a look of amazement and joy on his face.

Kendall stared at the rocket, the look in his eyes revealing a regret and longing that he knew could never be fully comprehended or fulfilled. He glanced down and spotted the ABORT button. Instinctively, he hastened his right hand toward then over it. But he did not press down. He just couldn't do that to his friend.

Tica pressed her hands over her face, fingers barely spread as she peered through the slits between them at the rocket.

Tears streamed down Christina's face. "ONE!!!!!!!!!!!" screamed Kendall.

As the rocket, and Jeremy's small, pale face, seemed to hover in mid-air, giving them a moment for a final farewell, Tica gave a wiggly-fingers wave. Grant's high-five turned into the famous split-fingered Dr. Spock salute. Christina blew a kiss then made a heart shape with her hands.

Jeremy shrugged his tiny shoulders and gave them a final, snaggle-toothed grin.

Kendall, shaking his head, muttered, "What have we done?"

As they pondered the answer to that question, the rocket gently lifted up into the night sky.

"WE HAVE LIFTOFF!!!!!" Grant shouted.

And they did. Miraculously, incredibly, flabbergastingly, the rocket gave a final quiver and began to rise. In the small window they watched the small face. It was beaming.

"Good luck, buddy," whispered Grant. "Sorry about the barf jokes."

ALL POINTS BULLETIN
IMMEDIATE ACTION REQUIRED!
HOUSTON POLICE DEPARTMENT

AN UNIDENTIFIED OBJECT SPOTTED OVER
JOHNSON SPACE CENTER.
POSSIBLE SABOTAGE JSC FACILITIES.
POSSIBLE LINK TO FIVE MISSING HOUSTON
TEENS. IMMEDIATE CONVERGENCE ON
AREA. CAUTION ADVISED. NASA SECURITY
IS PART OF THIS OPERATION. ALSO FBI,
CIA. RUN ALL OPS THRU SECTION R697B.
REPEAT: ALL OPS THRU SECTION R697B.
ADVISE EXTREME CAUTION!

The Mission Control door burst open and the room was invaded by soldiers and law officers. Once inside, they froze in place, unsure of what to do. It was clear to them that a manned space mission was actively in progress. Impossibly, it seemed to be in the control of a bunch of kids.

Frantic, now that the rocket was launched, Christina tried to turn into the CapCom. She always thought the astronaut would have stuck around for this role. After all, as she understood it, only an astronaut could talk to the crew aboard a rocket—probably even if that crew was just a little kid.

"Rules, schmools!" Christina swore to herself. She grabbed a headset and begged, "Jeremy? Jeremy? This is Mission Control. Please give us a report!"

No reply.

"Jeremy, I'm not kidding now. Let us know you're okay. A-OK. Please? Jeremy? *Jeremy?*" pleaded Christina, her voice cracking in spite of herself.

No reply.

"JEREMY!" Christina bellowed into the microphone. "This is a direct order from Mission Control. If your communication system is activated, immediately give us some sign that all is well up there...Roger that?" Christina was shaking. Everyone in the room stood still, staring up at the night sky and the diminishing light of the spacecraft. Everyone listened for even the faintest reply.

There was none.

With a quick glance around at the eyes of the other kids she could see that they, like her, were feeling perhaps a little envious, and left behind.

68

Outside, and around the corner of Mission Control, admiring the temporary clear hole in the night sky, the astronaut watched the rocket hover momentarily as it lifted off. If anyone could have seen him, seen his face, they would have said that he seemed to be both here...and there... and satisfied with each. With a tear in the corner of his eye, the astronaut, whispered, "Godspeed, young man, Godspeed."

The astronaut says:
The other night, when we were watching the stars together, Jeremy told me what Mob, his bear's name, meant. "It's really MOB, Mars or Bust," he said. "How long have you had him?" I asked, noticing that the bear was ragged and shaggy. "Since I was real little," he said. "My mom made him for me, uh, before, you know, before..." I said, "I understand."

69

As the soldiers and officers continued to stand ready, but fearful, to stop the action in progress in Mission Control, Tica couldn't help herself. She ran back to the PAO console and began to transmit:

"BLAST OFF!
NASA IS OPEN FOR BUSINESS!
MARS OR BUST!
EAT OUR DUST!"

That broke the spell. Suddenly, all heck broke loose. The soldiers went into action and chaos ensued.

"STAY WHERE YOU ARE!" shouted one soldier.

"You mean right here on Earth? Too late, guys!" Grant cried.

With shocked looks on their faces, the soldiers stared at the empty concrete bay and up into the night sky that was already streaking over with rain as the eye of the hurricane passed and the backside of the storm shoved over the area.

"THIS IS THE U.S. MARSHAL…STOP ALL MOVEMENTS…"

"SPECIAL OPS DEMANDS YOU STAND DOWN! STAND DOWN!! STAND DOWN NOW!!!"

"HOUSTON POLICE FORCE! PUT YOUR HANDS UP!"

"Uh, oh!" cried Tica. "Over and out from the Voice of Mission Control, cause I think I'm in a big mess…just send my bail to the Houston jail collection pail…"

A pair of powerful gloved hands lifted Tica from her seat as she squealed with bared teeth.

The other kids were petrified but strangely calm. All Christina could think of was that she was responsible for the launch, the rocket, the mission, and most especially, that small face in the window. She grabbed her console and stood firm, staring at the monitor. She continued her role as CapCom, or, rather, since she was not an astronaut herself, as a Capsule Communicator.

"Jeremy," she called over and over again, her voice growing weak with the repetition. "Jeremy, please respond. Jeremy, please respond…" until she realized that an automated computer voice had taken over:

DESTINY IS DOWN RANGE...static...
static...MILES
DESTINY IS TRAVELING AT...static...
static...static
DESTINY IS ON COURSE FOR...static...
static...

A soldier grabbed Christina under the arms and hauled her toward the door. She protested by wrapping her legs around her chair, which bought her a few seconds of time. She held tight to her headset as she continued to try to raise Jeremy.

Kendall stood his ground, too. He was so focused on the mission's progress that he ignored the soldier screaming at him. Like Christina, he stared at his console, focused on making heads or tails of what the readouts meant.

"Son! Do not resist!" a soldier screamed at Kendall for the second time. "We are taking you into custody. Stand down, son, stand down!"

In the back of his mind Kendall was aware that he and his friends were the cause of all this commotion. But it just didn't register with reality. To him, the fact that they had just launched an incredible new kind of rocket into space—with their friend aboard—was the only reality.

But so was this: a Houston police officer handcuffed Kendall's hands behind his back and pulled him to his feet.

As the soldiers each took hold of a child, everyone was startled when the automated voice filled the Mission Control room with this message:

DESTINY IS ON TRAJECTORY...
DESTINY IS ON TRAJECTORY...
DESTINY IS ON TRAJECTORY...FOR MARS...

The kids cheered as loudly as their now hoarse voices would allow.

"So that's what Jeremy was doing all this time!" Kendall shouted to the others, as he was dragged away.

"A flight plan for Mars!" Christina called back.

"No wonder he wanted to learn to cope with zero gravity barfity," said Grant, struggling with the lady soldier who had hauled him up so tightly that his short legs jiggled in the air. He rotated his feet as if riding a bike.

"Hey, you!" Grant hollered up at the soldier's pointed chin. "That's one small step for mankind, one giant leap BACKWARDS for me!" he cried as he weaseled his way out of the soldier's grip and fell onto the floor, only to be swooped back up and grasped so tightly that Grant cried, "Uncle!" In response, the soldier squeezed him even harder and Grant winced and gave up resisting.

Tica, teeth still bared, shouted, "I BITE! DADGUMMIT! I BITE!"

The three other kids hollered, "She does! She does!"

And when they heard a soldier screech...they knew that Tica had.

A late night television anchor, clearly excited to be the one to share breaking news of such a rare nature, blared:

"The president has authorized an emergency team of NASA mission experts to the Johnson Space Center to take over an apparent space flight currently in progress..."

As the newscaster spoke these words, a slew of former NASA employees, surrounded by security guards, spewed through the entrance gate and passed the kids headed out of the gate toward jail.

Even in the rush, glances were exchanged. The big-eyed, and much-relieved, kids caught all the nods of thanks, the low-handed high-fives, and the occasional grin from some of the workers and astronauts streaming in.

"They look excited," Tica called to Christina.

"They are intense, aren't they?" said Christina, noting the urgent body language propelling them into the building. "Men on a mission! Always were…hopefully always will be." She felt a wistful hollowness in her stomach and wondered how quickly she could get through school and join them. Back to the real world seemed so boring now.

As the last NASA guy passed, he stopped and stood in front of the kids, forcing them all—even the military—to stop in their tracks. He was an older, bald man with a big, loud Texan accent. "Just wahnted to say ya'll kids shore do have the rhaht stuff!" He grinned broadly, tipped his cowboy hat, and moved on.

And then the chaos of military, media, and general mayhem resumed and the kids were pushed into a large van that quickly sped away.

72

They were taken to police headquarters where there was barely-controlled chaos. Finally they were sorted momentarily into the five kids on one side of the squad room, and Carl Crispin and Joe Mast on the other.

"I think we've got some 'splainin' to do," guessed Grant. He was tired and hungry and needed to pee really bad. Where was a space diaper when you needed one!

"Dad!" cried Kendall, as he broke from the line and ran over to give his father a hug. "You're just here to pick us up, right?" All the kids watched for his answer, wondering why the two men were here if they'd managed to get away earlier before the authorities showed up.

Carl Crispin shook his head and gave his son an apologetic smile. "No, son. I have to admit—we ratted you guys out."

"WHAT?!" all the kids cried, shocked and not comprehending.

Joe Mast explained. "When we heard you in Mission Control, we knew you'd throttle up. We weren't far away, sort of keeping an eye out on you. But when we saw the propulsion steam we got scared. We realized that we'd taken advantage of you, and..."

"What do you mean?" asked Christina. "You did no such thing. You helped us. We'd already been there..." She stopped to look up at the officer in charge. "Uh, to do what we planned to do."

Joe Mast shook his head. "Yes, and we should have stopped you. Not because what you were doing was wrong. You kids were doing the right thing to try to get America back in space. As I heard Grant say, space belongs to you kids, but I guess you'll have to fight for it in Washington... like us adults."

"We were worried," added Carl Crispin. "We knew what the smoke and fire was, and we were thrilled the launch was going to come off—that was our reason for butting in and helping out, but our motives were selfish, too—trying to grab onto a past that's gone for us. We gotta accept it." He looked at Joe Mast. "We finally came to our senses and realized that you kids could get hurt, so, we, uh—sorry—called the authorities and headed back to the Center to make sure you were A-OK."

"Heyyyyy," said Grant. "Where is the, uh, the, uh, you-know-who?"

The men gave him a puzzled look.

Grant rolled his eyes. "Uh, you know, the, uh…THE ASTRONAUT?!"

"Yes," said Christina, "Is he OK? Did he get away?" She didn't know if she was more concerned that her special helper in Mission Control hadn't come back for them, or if he'd managed to get away.

Once more, Carl Crispin and Joe Mast exchanged puzzled glances. Joe Mast put his hands on his hips and shook his head. "We have no idea who you are talking about, kids."

At first the kids gave him a "Sure! Right! You forgot a real astronaut!" look. Then they realized that the men were probably covering for the astronaut to keep him from being in trouble like they were. But apparently, that was not so.

"Really, son," Carl Crispin added softly to Kendall. "We don't know what you mean. Is there something we should know?" He seemed very concerned.

Suddenly Grant burst into laughter. "I knew it!" he said. "I knew there were NASA ghosts. *Good* ghosts," he reminded himself. "Good ghosts of space past."

#

The kids were in a lot of trouble. The authorities took them all to a holding room to interrogate them about the "unidentified object spotted in the night sky," as the first news reporter on the scene had put it as he streamed coverage right from his cellphone to the station.

"But it's NOT unidentified!" Kendall said to the detective.

"Oh, yeah?" said the detective, glaring at the boy. "Well, it's sure as heck unauthorized, kid!"

"Oh, yeah, yourself!" said Grant, shoving himself between Kendall and the detective. "It was too AUTHORIZED."

"By who?" asked a cop, who stood tall and serious nearby, arms folded.

Instantly, the kids squirmed and inched their way together until they stood side-by-side, arms linked. They spread their legs and held their ground. Surrounded by puzzled, aggravated, threatening faces, they looked at each other and then up at the many officers glaring down at them.

"Authorized by who?" the chief officer demanded.

"By us!" Christina said, chin poked out.

Grant stood on tiptoe. "I mean somebody's gotta be in charge of space's future, tall dudes, and it looks like it might as well be us!" Tica and Kendall nodded like crazy.

It was a rare moment, when in spite of the sirens still raving outside and the incessant noise in the squad room, the adults themselves were speechless. That is until the chief officer said, "Well, kids, you'll just have to run the world...or space...or whatever it is you have in your weird little minds...from jail."

74

By the time Ms. Rodriguez and a couple of lawyers showed up and temporarily worked everything out, the backside of the hurricane had passed over Houston, been downgraded to a tropical storm, and moved on to pester Oklahoma.

As the kids walked out of the police station, weary, but happy, they gathered in a huddle beneath the now clear night sky.

"One day this will make a great movie," Kendall said.

"Yeah, only there weren't any special effects," groused Grant.

The other kids stared at him.

"No special effects?!" hollered Tica, raising her arms high and spinning round and round. She flung her arms at the night sky bowled above them and ordered, "LOOK! JUST LOOK AT 'EM!"

They all stared up at the massive array of stars and grinned. But each was seeing something different: those wild images from the Hubble Space Telescope...

scenes from all the space movies they'd ever watched…and their visions of the multiverse the astronaut had so vividly painted for them.

"WOW!" said Grant, staring up, and seeing all this night magic in one wild array overhead, walked smack into a light post. He never even felt the impact, just backed off, rubbed his forehead and kept on walking, eyes up to the sky, a big grin on his face.

Kendall smiled at Christina and took her hand.

Tica followed behind, hips swaying. "I guess I'll have to go into the Witness Protection Program, 'cause my mama's gonna kill me when she sees me on TV. And my grandma, boy, howdy, she will kill me twice."

"Tica, your grandmother is ninety-nine!" Christina reminded the girl.

Tica's big brown eyes gleamed in worry. "She *tough*."

Not far away, the astronaut stood in the shadows, shook his head, smiled, and silently tipped his hand against his helmet in salute.

75

The first day back at school, having turned in their report, Christina pondered what she had learned from this experience. As the astronaut had said, "It's always best to expect the unexpected." Being the oldest of the kids, she thought she'd be the one in charge. But she felt that no matter what she did, it was still the little things—good, bad, right, wrong, in-between, important or inconsequential—that really moved things along. Part teamwork, she could see that, but also some dumb luck, or luck based on doing more right than wrong, or good timing, or...well, she wasn't sure just what exactly; she had no name for this phenomenon, had never read about it in a book or learned it in a class. It made her wonder what else she didn't yet know that could come in handy in the real world, the adult world. It made her think of her parents' work with germs and how a deadly one could die out without doing any harm, while a harmless pathogen could adapt, change, and wreak havoc around the globe. It had all been so scary, fun, weird, known, unknown, good, bad, and nerve-wracking. She couldn't even say if it had all turned out OK. Being FLIGHT was just a name, a role—but she knew she'd at least tried to do her best. She felt older, and wiser. No, not wiser, she realized—but wise enough to know that wisdom was elusive. She thought being a responsible adult was sure going to be a challenge, especially when life and death, or fiery rockets, and such, were at stake. There was more to learning than book study, she thought. A lot more. She felt a new respect for adults, but tried to shrug that off. Time for that later, she thought. First, let's see what the adults do to us poor kids!

76

Later that night, as Christina sat on her bed in the dark, still pondering all that had happened to them, she felt so confused. On the one hand, she felt good about some things—especially about getting out of jail and being back home. She was especially relieved that her parents (though they didn't actually say so) seemed to almost be proud of her and Grant. It made Christina realize that her parents hadn't always been old—they were in their forties, for goodness sake—but had once been young, and maybe even dare-devilish?

On the other hand, she didn't understand the astronaut. Had they imagined him? How could he be the good guy she suspected he was, yet let them launch their friend into space? While she struggled with staying awake and thinking about the moral implications of this, her iPhone beeped and an eerie green backlit message appeared. It read:

Sorry, Christina. Hope you are not disappointed in me.

I forgot to tell you that Jeremy has his SOCKS and SHOES with him.
It was part of the payload.

Puzzled, Christina hoped someone wasn't playing a joke on her. Suspicious, she texted back:

Payload? SOCKS? SHOES?

In a moment, a new text arrived:

SOCKS: Simple Optimized Colonization Kit Single.
SHOES: Simple Help Onboard Extra-vehicular Scooter
When Jeremy lands he will have everything he needs. I promise.
After that, it's all up to him.

Christina was stunned. Tears brimmed in her eyes. *Lands*, she thought? *Where? When? How?* But all she texted back, with trembling fingers, was:

Who is this?

For quite a while, Christina thought there would be no answer. Then came:

You know.

And that was the last that she ever heard from the astronaut.

In the cool, cool, cool of the evenin'…
Tell 'em I'll be there…

Inside the tiny capsule, Jeremy gazed out at the stars and sang this refrain over and over in a small voice. He gazed at Earth and gave a little wave to his friends back there. He snuggled Mob in the crook of his arm. He had never known such happiness.

JOHNSON SPACE CENTER: It was announced today at Johnson Space Center, by the President of the United States, alongside the head of NASA and a number of former and current astronauts, that "An entirely new and dramatic era in American space flight has been approved by Congress and begins now! To explore deep space and all the opportunities that lie waiting for us there, we announce the launch of an entirely new kind of spacecraft. The first of these will launch by the first of the coming year. The first capsule to leave Earth and inaugurate this new era will be named...Jeremiah.

Tica became a paleophysicist, a fashion designer, and a part-time radio personality, with her own show, "Cool Science."

Kendall went into the military and distinguished himself in something called WMD-D, or Weapons of Mass Destruction *Destruction*. He was later awarded a Nobel Prize for Peace for this work.

Christina is the author of popular science fiction books under the series title *Smoke from a Distant Star*.

Carl Crispin and Joe Mast testified before a Congressional hearing to investigate whether the U.S. should reinstate its quest into deep space and the colonization of Mars. For NASA, they secretly continued to monitor the flight of the real "first" of the new rockets.

Grant is a fourth-grade science teacher at a Houston elementary school. Two of his former students would go on to become astronauts on the MCM, the Mars Colonization Mission. He started a scholarship for space camps for underprivileged children in a foundation called Jeremy's Universe.

When the first "official" Mars Colonization Mission spacecraft was launched, they were all invited to watch the launch.

Once a year, on a certain date in September, Christina, Kendall, Grant, and Tica meet near an ugly green dumpster at Johnson Space Center with a bottle of champagne and four glasses, to toast their former friend, wherever he may be.

One morning, months later, a NASA employee at Johnson Space Center noticed a blue light burning on the Top Secret/ Classified/EYES ONLY *Destiny* monitor. *"Contact!"* he whispered, mostly to himself, then to the two other men working nearby, "CONTACT! We have a blue contact light on *Destiny*...a blue cockpit light confirming that it's landed. *LANDED!"*

80

In his old age, in a nursing home, a former security guard at a building next to the Johnson Space Center rambled on and on about a boy he met one day long ago. He told his nurse, "I always wondered what happened to that crazy kid who swore he and his friends had taken over NASA and were going to launch a rocket into space!" He slapped his now skinny and withered thigh and laughed a throaty cough. "Did you ever hear of such a tall tale?"

"We have a long way to go in this space race. But this is the new ocean, and I believe that the United States must sail on it and be in a position second to none."—President John F. Kennedy, to Joint Session of Congress, May 25, 1961

Acknowledgments

This is my first effort at writing a kind of, sort of bridge book from my 100 Carole Marsh Mysteries (for ages 7-14) to a more Young Adult format. I'm not so keen on all these labels. I read *On the Beach* when I was seven and enjoyed it immensely, so I trust readers to read what they want and like without a lot of help from (what I consider unnecessary) marketing "tags." My least favorite thing in the world is to see a young child, perhaps 10 or 11, perusing books in the adult section on the Civil War, quantum mechanics, or almost anything else…and see an adult show up and admonish them, "Those books are too old, too hard for you." Really? (Alas, this happens all the time in bookstores and libraries.)

However, while my first attempt may not be as good as my fifteenth attempt at so-called Tween or YA, it is certainly better because of these people:

First, thanks to the many fine space and science writers who often do a great job at making the complex exceedingly accessible and understandable. There are too many great books to name.

Second, my great appreciation to the Gallopade staff and freelancers—whom I call my A-Team—for their various participations in getting the manuscript ready for a tight publication schedule:

Paige Muh, my key grip, best boy, right hand gal, and otherwise do-the-impossible on a daily basis—you're what every writer needs!

Janice Baker, who helped with plot ideas, editing, finding maps, wrangling the whole mess, and otherwise improving every manuscript she touches.

Randolyn Friedlander and I had a great time working on the most intriguing look we could give this book (within small press time and budget constraints); thanks for all the ideas and great execution.

John Hanson, thanks for the use of your son as the star (to me) of this book, as well as all your high-magnitude talents in getting my books "right," whether in print or electronic formats.

To Gabrielle Humphrey, my great appreciation for taking a "mess" and fine-tooth-combing all the science and NASA facts.

To Anna Reuter for the fun photo shoot in the alley, and the cover shot in the office. Thank you for your patience, creativity, charm, and skill—especially since it was about one hundred degrees and you were nine months pregnant! (You could name the baby Nasa?) Also thanks to Paige for gathering characters, props, and talent, and so much more. Every day's an adventure, hey?

To Vicki Dejoy for the cover design; it's always a pleasure working with you!

My thanks to the entire Gallopade Team for everything from sales and marketing to publicity and, especially, putting money in the bank for me. (Always love that part!) Publishing is a complex world of a nanonillion details and your can- and will-do attitude always amazes me.

Also, I would like to thank the many independent bookstores and school supply/teacher stores whose personnel so aptly hand-sell, as they say, my books. Without you, as well as teachers, librarians, and reviewers—I'm not sure how readers would ever connect with the books just meant for them at the right time. No "Hey, kid, this book is too old/hard for you" ever comes from your lips. Bless you!

Thanks to Forrest Schultz for taking a fresh look at my recent books and helping me have more confidence to see things in them that I didn't even know were there!

More thanks than is possible is due my son and daughter, Michael Longmeyer and Michele Yother, who always have the Right Stuff!

And, last but not least, to Bob—Robert Longmeyer—my husband, the Cowboy Pilot, who would fly me to the Moon if I asked him to. Oh, he did!

And also:

NASA folks—past, present, and future: We all love you. I believe that in the rear view mirror of history one day, the best story will be that of America as a leader in space, not the race or the ups, downs, disasters, blips—but the beauty of perseverance, determination, and success that will surely exceed all we can possibly imagine. The Right Stuff indeed!

Any success ya'll all please take credit for. Any errors are mine alone.

Carole Marsh (Longmeyer)
Peachtree City, Georgia
September 2011

Newfangled Space Words and Terms

dark energy: although no one has ever seen it, it is believed it makes up about 70% of the universe; scientist are not sure what it is or where it comes from but believe it is the cause of the universe's expansion at an ever-increasing rate

dark matter: the invisible unknown "stuff" in space between stars; may make up a quarter of the universe; we know dark matter exists because it exerts a gravitational pull strong enough to hold galaxies together; however, it is not made of atoms and does not reflect light or any other kind of radiation

exobiology: the study of extraterrestrial environments for living organisms

exoplanet: a planet outside of Earth's solar system

geostationary: a circular orbit directly above Earth's equator; altitude 22,300 miles above Earth, where the speed of an object matches Earth's rotation so that the object remains stationary over the same point on Earth (see space elevator) *multiverse:* some scientists believe that there may be many other universes, possibly including some that have yet to inflate, or that have completely different physical laws and dimensions from ours

refueling depot: possible "gas stations" in space so that spacecraft do not need to haul all the fuel they would require for distant space travel

sailcraft: a form of propulsion where wafer-thin sails use the accumulative pressure of sunlight to move a spacecraft through space

solar electric: a potential type of rocket propulsion system

space elevator: the concept of a cable between Earth and a space station, via which you could transport cargo

terraforming: creating an Earthlike environment on another planet or moon

Interesting Resources

Good Space Places

www.nasa.gov
www.seds.org
www.space.com

NASA's television channel (check your local station listings)

Kennedy Space Center, Florida
National Air and Space Museum, Washington, DC
Rose Center for Earth and Space Science, New York City
Space Center Houston, Houston, Texas
U.S. Space and Rocket Center, Huntsville, Alabama

Good Space Books and Publications

Barlowe's Guide to Extraterrestrials by Wayne Douglas Barlowe,
Ian Summers, and Beth Meacham

Packing for Mars by Mary Roach

*The Mercury 13: The Untold Story of Thirteen American Women
and the Dream of Space Flight* by Martha Ackman

The Right Stuff by Tom Wolfe

Air & Space Magazine
Discover Magazine
Sky & Telescope Magazine

Out of This World Space Careers

Astronomer
Galactic astronomer
Planetary astronomer
Radio astronomer
Space biologist
Space chemist
Space geologist
Astrogeologist
Astronautical engineer
Astrochemist
Astrophysicist
Capsule communicator (CapCom)
Rocket scientist
Propulsion systems specialist
Space scientist
Simulation supervisor
Aeronautical engineer
Aerospace engineer
Computer programmer
Computer scientist
Electrical engineer
Fire protection engineer
Space materials engineer
Space mechanical engineer
Nuclear scientist
Plastics engineer
Robotics engineer
Safety engineer
Software systems tester
Mathematician
Systems analyst
Astronaut
Space technical writer
Archaeoastronomer
Cosmologist
Astrobiologist
Planetary scientist

About the Author

Carole Marsh has been writing for more than 30 years, producing both fiction and nonfiction books for children. Her latest literary endeavor launches Marsh's writing in a new direction, into the world of literature exploring the interests of a group of slightly older readers, young adolescents. As CEO of Gallopade International, she has made a career of communicating with kids and has produced what amounts to a library of educational products and books. Marsh is best known for her nationally-acclaimed mystery series, **Real Kids! Real Places!,** and her work has been recognized with awards from the Georgia Writers Association, iParenting Media, *Learning Magazine*, National School Supply & Equipment Association, Associations Advance America, and *Publisher's Weekly*. The author is married to Bob Longmeyer. They have two grown children who work with them in their business and five grandchildren who often serve as characters in her books. The author and her husband live in Peachtree City and Savannah, Georgia.

Hey, kids, Thanks for reading!

THROTTLE UP!
ALWAYS THROTTLE UP!

WHEN KIDS TAKE OVER NASA

READING GUIDE

Questions from Carole Marsh:

•When the space shuttle program ended in 2011, did you even care? Why or why not?

•Have you ever asked your parents or grandparents their opinions about space and what might have intrigued them over the years?

•Did you ever want to be an astronaut? Work at NASA? Go to space?

•Why do you think these five kids did what they did? Were they in over their heads? What word would you use to describe them? Were they renegades, reckless, or caught in that in-between age when you aren't allowed to do stuff, but you have to do stuff to move forward and grow up? Ever had that feeling?

•Can you identify a character trait in each kid character that served a purpose in the story? If it took a team to do this, what did each bring to the table? How did you feel that they slowly morphed into older and wiser during the story and more like a real team, more mature, and grew right in front of your eyes as the pressure of their challenge progressed?

•Why were Grant and Kendall often at odds with each other? Did Grant look up to Kendall? And did Kendall end up looking up to Grant? Were they really the same boy, only different ages, in some way?

•How did the relationship between Christina and Kendall change from rivalry to understanding, even friendship, companionship and likemindedness?

•Which character did you most identify with? In what ways and why?

•Is growing up a small step, giant leap, or both? Is it a straight line or a zigzag? A maze or a convoluted path? Use your own description; draw it; put an X on the spot where you feel you are at this time.

•Was the astronaut real? Do you think I know? Do you think I knew when I first added him to the story?

•Jeremy: What was his motivation to go to space? Was this his destiny or did he just choose it for himself? Did you see that coming? Do you think I suffered over sending him up, perhaps never to return? Do you wonder where he is now?

•Do you think there is any symbolism in the following things in the story? If so, what, and hey, there are no wrong answers, hint, hint!: The big old Johnson Space Center building…the Mission Control room…the maze of fences and areas that surrounded the Johnson Space Center…the forays out into the neighborhood…other?

•How much research do you think I did on the future possibilities in rocket research, propulsion, alternate physics, multiverses, etc.? Do you think I was surprised that there are really a LOT more ideas than I suspected and that some are moving right along, or were, at NASA and other places?

•Should I write a sequel? (Please say "No!"... I'm exhausted...but if you think "YES!" then email carole@gallopade.com and let me know! Vote for one of the titles in the list of Forthcoming Books in the front of this book, or suggest another WHEN KIDS TAKE OVER...title!)

•Hey, do you think there should be a movie? I DO!